A debut full of heart and energy, by an intense, fervent writer whose dedication shows in every line.

George Saunders, author of *Tenth of December: Stories*

This is a collection full of lingering stories and lovely lines, and it introduces Vickers as a vital new writer. His stories occupy a unique middle zone between the memorably bizarre and the movingly sweet-hearted, the deeply felt and the dementedly funny. He's also a tireless stylist, capturing his characters' sad-sack vernacular and tweaking every sentence until it yields some tongue-twisting lyricism.

Bennett Sims, author of *A Questionable Shape*

The stories are linked, by place, by time, by characters, by small events and large tragedies that pop up in brief mentions in one story and then disappear for several pieces, only to reappear and be examined from different perspectives more fully. The end effect is a set of connected stories that has the power of a novel and a magnetic, almost hypnotic pull on the reader.

Paul Griner, author of *Hurry Please I Want to Know*

Zachary Tyler Vickers's *Congratulations on Your Martyrdom!* is delightfully metafictive, admirably invested in social critique, and wisely aware of both the benefits and pitfalls of domestic verisimilitude. The interconnected nature of the stories allows Vickers to manage complex and complete world-building. An interesting and original addition to the canon of gonzo fiction!

Josh Russell, author of *Yellow Jack*

CONGRATULATIONS ON YOUR MARTYRDOM!

break away b🚲ks

INDIANA UNIVERSITY PRESS

Bloomington & Indianapolis

Congratulations on your Martyrdom!

Zachary Tyler Vickers

This book is a publication of

INDIANA UNIVERSITY PRESS
Office of Scholarly Publishing
Herman B Wells Library 350
1320 East 10th Street
Bloomington, Indiana 47405 USA

iupress.indiana.edu

The paper used in this publication
meets the minimum requirements of
the American National Standard for
Information Sciences – Permanence of
Paper for Printed Library Materials,
ANSI Z39.48–1992.

Manufactured in the
United States of America

Library of Congress
Cataloging-in-Publication Data

Vickers, Zachary Tyler.
[Short stories. Selections]
Congratulations on your
martyrdom! / Zachary Tyler Vickers.
pages cm. – (Break away books)
ISBN 978-0-253-01981-3
(pbk. : alk. paper) – ISBN 978-
0-253-01985-1 (ebook)
I. Title.
PS3622.I2837A6 2016
813'.6 – dc23

2015028891

1 2 3 4 5   21 20 19 18 17 16

FOR MY PARENTS

You forget that a thing is not necessarily true
because a man dies for it.

Oscar Wilde, "The Portrait of Mr. W. H."

CONTENTS

Acknowledgments

Thank you to Sam Chang and the Iowa Writers' Workshop for allowing me the time to write this book, to grow, and for all of the wonderful things you provided me, in head and heart. And to Deb, Jan, and Connie – thank you for all of your help and kindness. Thank you to all of my peers, in and out of workshop, who helped shape many of these stories.

To all of my teachers: Michelle Huneven, Allan Gurganus, Jim McPherson, Elizabeth McCracken, Ethan Canin, Alexander Chee, and Robin Hemley. To Michael Martone, of course: *i zoi!* To George Saunders: a mentor in humbleness and generosity, above and beyond your tutelage. To Jason Ockert: the first dude who showed me what fiction can really do – in his workshops and in his own stories – your classes changed my life, sir.

To my agent, Janet Silver, for all of her steadfast belief, support, and effort. To Sarah Jacobi and the entire staff at Break Away Books and Indiana University Press. And to all of the editors who published some of these stories in your incredible journals: *Emerson Review, Waccamaw, Spork, Hobart, American Reader, KGB Bar Lit Magazine, LVNG,* and *H-NGM-N.*

To all of my friends, again and again and again.

And to my family for all of their love, support, and encouragement. Especially to my brother, Colby; mother, Vicky; and father, Dave – you never blinked once when I set out to do this seemingly impossible thing. Thank you, thank you, thank you. I love you all.

Congratulations on YOUR MARTYRDOM!

DISFIGURED PAPER ANIMALS

I'm inserting the Magical Foam Organs into a Stuff-A-Bear ground-hog when Eddie calls me over to a bin of miscellaneous carcasses and asks if I require a warm baseball mitt to play with my pud. He laughs and makes his hand do a jack-off motion with these long lanky fingers like wolverines'. I tuck my hands into my pockets.

Eddie restocks the carcass bins. He recently got married after doing time for lashing somebody with a sock of oranges. He has been extra jerky since Burlington Kids Zoo Outlet opened at the other end of the mall, meaning he hasn't had as much to restock. We've avoided pay cuts and layoffs by switching to authentic carcasses that Shâbner buys cheap off Eddie's pal Uncle Angelo, the crooked Guido taxidermist. The few customers we get haven't noticed. They choose a limp carcass from a bin and bring it to me for Life-Giving. I insert Magical Foam Organs, stuff it with a hose called the Umbilical Cord, then close it up with a colorful threaded suture. After that it goes to Blind Chris for Bathing – a station with a miniature claw-footed basin and air hose. Then the Stuff-A-Bear transfers to Attire for clothing and accessories. Then it's off to Shâbner at the register for Payment/Birth Certificate.

Eddie is still laughing as I finish the groundhog. My stitching is flawless. My fat hands keep the carcass straight on the sewing ma-chine. But that's all they're good for. Because of my short stubby fin-gers, it's a challenge to even grip a spoon or palm a softball. I've heard my share of ridicule. I could get an operation to thin and lengthen my fingers, but I can't afford something like that. It's easier just to keep my hands in my pockets.

*   *   *

Midday, Shâbner announces a staff meeting, holding what looks like a mutilated Stuff-A-Bear bunny. It must've been geeky Hal Winkler, manager of Burlington Kids Zoo Outlet. He and Shâbner have been warring for stuffed animal distributor supremacy. Notches have been upped back and forth. Lately, Winkler has been snooping around, sending us Polaroids of Stuff-A-Bears S&Ming each other: ball-gagged and paddled and choke-collared. Shâbner countered by filling a BKZO chimp with Bangzo FireCracklers, which Eddie set off in Winkler's office trash can. The war has upped another notch since.

We convene in the stockroom. Blind Chris has his hands on the card table like two pale carnations, folding another piece of colored paper. Eddie mocks me by sucking a knuckle. It reminds me of my last date at the Cineplex. I wore the usual driving gloves and finger extensions. The woman, Gwynn, twisted her blonde hair with a red-nailed finger. I should've known when she ran one of those red nails up my thigh and purred at the sight of the *Coming Attractions*. As soon as the lights dimmed, she began to claw at my belt and pants, her nose whistling from a deviated septum. I begged her to watch the movie but she was in a severe heat. Her whistles were high and quick and wanting. She removed one of my driving gloves and ended up suckling one of the finger extensions. It fell from her tongue and bounced a few rows down. She gagged, stood, left me staring at the screen. I don't recall the flick. I'm sure it was the type where the Happily Ever After doesn't quite happen, and all the lovesick ponies in the audience go home with nothing in their lungs to cheer about.

"BKZO has upped things another notch!" Shâbner shouts. He shows us the mangled Stuff-A-Bear: an arm in a cast, a purple ring painted around a button eye. Pinned to its chest is a Polaroid of a food court saltshaker. *You cheat!* is written on the back. After a series of instigating emails, Shâbner and Winkler met in the food court for a staring contest. Shâbner won by allegedly flicking salt from the shaker into Winkler's eye.

"We need to take things up yet another notch!" Shâbner exclaims. He motivates himself again by sharing the photograph of his laughing wife. She'd leave him for sure if she knew Marshall's college fund had been nearly depleted to invest in the Stuff-A-Bear franchise. He's been trying to earn it back. He shows us his knotty bruised shins where Marshall has kicked him because he can't afford to host his sixth birthday party at the PizzaPalace.

Shâbner motivates us. He asks Blind Chris, did he enjoy walking dogs? Blind Chris again replies, "No." There was nothing enjoyable about rabies shots in the stomach. Blind Chris's purple paper is taking shape. Maybe it's a goat.

Shâbner turns to Eddie. How else would he have met his wife? Eddie shrugs. He met her when she was just another scarce customer browsing the BrokenHeart Bears, a bruise sitting up high on her cheek like a lullaby. Eddie wooed her by visiting her ex with a sock of oranges. They exchanged vows after he made parole for good behavior.

"And you," Shâbner says to me. "Remember how I took you in as a wee dropout? Where would you be without Stuff-A-Bear?" I shrug. I've worked here since high school. My fingers are too stubby to type or grip a hammer. But I can sew, and for decent pay. Otherwise, my résumé is as useful as a paper airplane. When I think about life without Stuff-A-Bear, I imagine slumming around the dollar theater beside old high school faces, nostalgic about nothing, cigarettes between our chapped, underachieving lips.

No way I'm doing that.

"What do we do?" Blind Chris asks. He reminiscently touches his stomach and frowns, cradling his purple deformed crane – one wing larger than the other; the head just a giant beak. Still, it's impressive. I'd like to learn something like that. Practice such grace despite these hands of mine, these fingers like stocky bastard children.

"We're going to dress a BKZO zebra up like a prostitute and plant it in Hal Winkler's office!" Shâbner says and raises a mail-ordered zebra. Eddie cracks his neck. Blind Chris flares his nostrils and nods. I keep my hands in my pockets.

Shâbner volunteers me to buy some lingerie. I put on my finger extensions and driving gloves and pick out the skimpiest item at LuckyLadies Boutique, near the food court. The sexy cashier mentions that I made a fine choice. She arches her back and says the recipient must be someone very special. I blush, shrug, look away.

The BKZO zebra gets sewn into the lingerie with *Skank!* written in sequins across the backside. Shâbner gives a thumbs-up to this and tells me I have impeccably poor taste. Red lipstick gets smeared on the zebra's mouth for extra skankiness. We head to the other end of the mall, where the tornado recently ripped the roof off the department store. Anabolix gym is covered with tarps, in repair. Its sign reads COMING SOON! and I think of Gwynn. The hole in the far wall is from a fifty-pound dumbbell hurled through the Sheetrock. It looks like the hole Eddie once punched in the bathroom stall. At Burlington Kids Zoo Outlet, Eddie tiptoes inside with the zebra under his shirt. Moments later he exits the store without it. We wait behind the wishing fountain until we hear Hal Winkler's nasally shriek. He stomps out. Shâbner meets him toe-to-toe and they stare at each other, mumbling *Why I Oughtas!* Then Shâbner blinks. Winkler snorts victoriously and jogs away. Shâbner slumps.

"Meeting adjourned," he grumbles.

*   *   *

Over the weekend I decide to borrow an origami book from the library. The evening air is thrilling. The falsetto croaks of peepers sidle through my trailer's kitchen window. I sit at the table and start with a simple hopping frog. But it's difficult. I recall the nickname ThimbleFists. My soft fingertips can't press crisp folds into the construction paper. My hopping frog ends up looking more like a crumpled wad of green paper.

Grammie described my hands as the manifestations of impure thoughts. But before the cobwebs, she mentioned it was genetic, gathering enough lucidity to recount Pop's hands as *fleshy oven mitts*. He and Ma died in a plane crash. Pop was piloting. They were honeymooning. I was infantile. Grammie was babysitting. Sometimes I wonder if the plane crashed because of Pop's inability to grip the controls.

Children crouch in the trailer park weeds and strike each other with Wiffle ball bats. I try folding another hopping frog. The smell of warm asphalt reminds me of pickup games as a boy, back before my hands grew out of me and a bat was easier to grip. Back before the ridicule when I was just another delighted face watching the Drums Along the Mohawk parade each summer. But as my hands swelled, my childhood wept and fled, and I found myself pushed back in the crowd until the parade seemed like it was for everybody but me.

The next hopping frog turns out better. I crack my knuckles and try again.

*   *   *

On Monday, Shâbner meets Hal Winkler by the escalators, where they shake fists at each other for a good period of time. More

5

authentic raccoon, squirrel, rabbit, and beaver carcasses arrive while he is gone. They're just as cuddly as the synthetic fiber fur ones, but they're also borderline hideous. It usually takes a few hours to adjust the carcasses – remove the teeth and claws with pliers and replace the beady glass eyes with cute buttons. I don't think about where they come from. The other night, I saw a news report about a local pet store robbery. I shut off the television, convinced myself it was nothing, not related to us, remembering how it could be worse: ratcheting stop signs with the old high school faces or rewinding videotapes manually with a twist of my stumpy pointer finger wedged into one of the reels. I tell myself the animals are already dead. I didn't kill them. But a lump lingers in my gut. Sometimes when the lump feels too big, I pretend that I really am giving life back to the carcasses, a second chance.

In every batch we get defects: limbless or rancid. Eddie discards these in the loading dock dumpster. When he returns, he tapes something to my back. I reach around and pull off a sign that reads NUB-BINS. He laughs and sucks a knuckle. I consider slapping his face and leaving little red nubbin marks. But it's not wise to get Eddie's teakettle whistling. One time he got a traffic ticket and trashed the stockroom with a tire iron. Then there was the time Hal Winkler sent us a Polaroid of Eddie picking his nose, and he punched a hole in the bathroom stall. Or when a bird shat on his head as he came into work, and he followed the fluttering thing back to its tree, knocked its nest down, and stomped the eggs. Shâbner has focused Eddie's quote-unquote "unbiased fervor for life" on the notch-upping war against Hal Winkler.

So instead of slapping his face and leaving little red nubbin marks and whistling his teakettle, I fold frogs on my car dashboard during lunch. The callus on my pointer finger helps sharpen each crease. I make a new model: an ugly yellow whale.

Returning to work, I pass the loading dock. A cloud of flies figure-eights above it while Hal Winkler leans in, clicking his camera. "Hey!" I shout. He looks up and adjusts his big geeky glasses. I flip him the bird and he chuckles at my pudgy little obscenity. I make like I'm going to chase after him and he takes off, weaving between cars in the parking lot.

I give life to more Stuff-A-Bears. I pretend to stuff myself by placing the Umbilical Cord to my bellybutton and puffing my cheeks. Kids giggle. Parents give me pervert looks. Nobody snickers because I'm wearing my driving gloves and finger extensions. Shâbner returns from lunch and compliments my work ethic with a big thumbs-up. But his good mood sours when I tell him about Hal Winkler snapping Polaroids around the dumpster.

"Shit, oh shit!" he says.

Eddie and I follow him out to the loading dock to discard the defective carcasses into the gully stream. The cloud of flies has disappeared. The smell of trash hangs in the humidity and smothers us. We peer into the dumpster. Shâbner covers his eyes. Eddie kicks the loading dock door. The defective carcasses are gone.

* * *

I go to the state park beach and find a warm plot near the boardwalk, watching the Rollerbladers and bums slowly burn. Across the lake, the palisades loom. Kids called the trees along its bluffed top "The Spot." They'd drink and hump and sometimes dive into the lake below until one boy cannonballed into a passing motorboat. They never found his body. Now the palisades are fenced off and plastered with warnings.

I fold an orange ballerina, a yellow bee, a pink rose. The ballerina's head is too large, the bee's wings aren't symmetrical, and the rose is missing petals. I think maybe the hand surgery might give me the ability to fold quality models. A paper rose would look nice pinned to my shirt. Maybe I could use it to woo Emily at StickyBunz Bakery in the food court. I wear my driving gloves and finger extensions whenever I order, and she always greets me with a cheery "Hello, handsome! Would you like to try a strawberry crepe?" I like how she calls me *handsome*. I think *strawberry crepe* really means something more. Maybe a quality paper rose would help discover what that is. Maybe she has webbed feet and will kiss my thick knuckles in sympathy. Maybe I'll massage her flippers. Maybe we'll make love and exorcise our loneliness under a yolky moon that hangs low like a naked motel room lightbulb.

Maybe. Maybe not.

I like the intricate folds of an advanced dragon in the back of the book. I give it a try. But it's not long before my hands cramp and I crumple the paper. I fold a unicorn instead. But after the unicorn, I retry the dragon. I get further this time. A tail begins to take shape. Then it ruins and I toss it in the trash, where a bum is looking for soda cans.

* * *

Later in the week, protesters march and picket outside Stuff-A-Bear, chanting, "Go stuff yourselves!" They raise enlarged photographs of the defective carcasses placed in their natural habitats: a squirrel draped over a tree branch, a raccoon lying on a garbage can, a beaver sunbathing on some rocks beside the gully stream, a rabbit in the grass birthing colorful Easter eggs. News reporters document everything. They ask us questions. We don't comment. Shâbner finds a Polaroid under his windshield wiper: the rabbit carcass in the grass with the Easter eggs. A note on the back reads: *Do You Know Where*

Your Pet Is? Shop Burlington Kids Zoo Outlet and Leave the Beef to the Butchers!

Shâbner says, "Shit, oh shit, oh shit!"

We close early and replace all of the authentic carcasses with the few synthetics in storage. Uncle Angelo stops by – this big ape with a tuft of silver chest hair creeping out of his shirt, chewing a fat cigar, probably to keep from saying too much. His taxidermy shop was rumored to have illegal gambling, moonshine, stuffed cock fighting. But the evidence vanished and the prosecution's only witness was found in his bathtub cradling a toaster.

After mall security breaks up the protest, Uncle Angelo loads the authentic carcasses into his sea-foam Caddy. Shâbner fears this is the übernotch. He rubs his shins and mutters, "Forgive me, Marshall! Upstate Community College isn't *so* bad!" Uncle Angelo hawks a loogie, lights a new cigar, and makes his face squash and narrow.

Eddie arrives late from a dentist appointment. When he discovers what has happened, he kicks over the Magical Foam Organs bin. He says he won't go back. They'll never get him behind bars again alive. He's about to break the Umbilical Cord over his knee when Uncle Angelo whispers into his ear. Eddie's brow scrunches.

"We'll fix this for good," he grunts.

"Another übernotch?" Shâbner asks.

"The überest," Eddie says.

Then Eddie and Uncle Angelo climb into the sea-foam Caddy and drive off.

In the meantime, Shâbner says we need to salvage Stuff-A-Bear's reputation. We stamp all the synthetic carcasses with the words *Genuine Imitation*. We hang a picture at the storefront of a bunny family dancing in a field of daisies. We make small donations to a series of animal shelters and list them all in a brochure labeled "Friends of Stuff-A-Bear."

We open the store back up. But nobody comes in.

Later we find a Polaroid taped to the loading dock door portraying Eddie and myself adjusting the authentic carcasses. *Tisk tisk!* is written on the back. Eddie is gluing on button eyes and I'm pulling out the teeth of a puppy carcass. My tongue hangs in concentration. The lump in my gut balloons when I think of the puppy ghost's gummed muzzle begging me to *thtop thtop thtop.* At what point did I decide this was an okay thing to do?

Then I look at my hands and remember.

Blind Chris and I pick up the spilled Magical Foam Organs. I wonder if that puppy ever had an owner who called its name from the front porch. I shake the thought and notice a purple paper crane in Blind Chris's shirt pocket. I ask him how he learned origami. He tells me his grandmother – she would move his hands over each fold until he memorized the steps. Her hands, gentle as tissue. He only remembers how to make cranes now. I try to imagine Grammie doing something like that but only recall how she prayed for me over a cup of coffee and a cigarette late when the summer frost crawled over the windowpane.

I ask Blind Chris if he ever wonders what the paper cranes look like.

"No," he replies. "For me, it's not about what they look like at all."

*   *   *

I fold a hornless dragon. I make some poor pink roses and yellow whales. Then I think about what Blind Chris said. I close my eyes, feel for a piece of paper, and attempt a hopping frog. Even with my eyes shut I can visualize each step, every crease. A new, exciting feeling builds in my chest. The end result resembles a hopping frog. The flaws feel right but I don't know why, and I don't have time to consider them more because my front door kicks in and some masked mugger enters with a golf club. I reach for the phone but can't dial 911. My fat fingers press too many numbers at once, and all I can do is curse them and cover my face as the mugger raises the golf club with these long lanky fingers like wolverines'.

He thrusts the golf club down.

There is an obnoxious thud in my brain and everything goes black.

* * *

My skull throbs. I'm sitting in a chair, hands tied behind me. My eyes begin to adjust, and I notice all the torture machines and mounted animal heads.

Somebody sits to my left. I squint and recognize Hal Winkler's geeky glasses. He looks thinner than I remember. I whisper to him, but he doesn't flinch. My eyes adjust more. I notice that he's naked. I ask, "Why are you naked?" Nothing. Then my eyes adjust even more. I see the large gash in his chest, the newspapers wedged in to keep him upright. He has no eyes, and his jaw just hangs open so it looks like he's laughing in that way dead people do.

My thick fingers tremble.

Footsteps clunk down the staircase.

Eddie squats in front of me. It's simple, he tells me. Winkler has made quite a mess for all of us. Jail isn't an option. He's got someone to provide for now. Either I'm going to be part of the solution or part of the problem. What am I going to be?

"Part of the solution," I say.

Eddie nods, "Then you need to stuff him."

"What?" I say.

"We need the evidence to disappear. There's a black market for decoy bodies in the Middle East. You know how to use the Umbilical Cord and sewing machine. Your cut will be five hundred. Just think of him as a big teddy bear," Eddie says, flicking a spider from a web in Hal Winkler's mouth. Behind him, Uncle Angelo puffs, and his cigar cherries bright.

I imagine Hal Winkler half buried in the desert getting picked at by vultures and scorpions, or shot at by warring sects. His ghost plays fetch with the toothless puppy ghost and he mentions, "What an unfortunate notch this is!"

But five hundred bucks could be a down payment on that surgery. No more stupid driving gloves and finger extensions. No more hands in pockets. I could ask out Emily at StickyBunz Bakery. Hal Winkler is already dead. I didn't kill him. I just have to stuff him. Somebody is going to do it for five hundred bucks. Why can't it be me? Why can't I get ahead in life? I can. But I have to *stuff* Hal Winkler.

"What's it going to be?" Eddie asks. I begin to sweat.

"I don't know," I say. "I don't know, I don't know, I don't know."

"Then you're going to be part of the problem, Jimbo," Eddie says and duct-tapes a Magical Foam Organ into my mouth. I'm surprised and almost flattered by the sound of my actual-sort-of name coming out of him. I can taste the velvety surface of the Magical Foam Organ heart, pumping with regret. Uncle Angelo reveals a very large knife from his belt. I squirm and rethink my answer while blue light glints off the blade. Cigar smoke bleeds up over his face as if his breath is burning. His silver tuft of chest hair sings to me. His strong aftershave gets in a few jabs. I don't want to die. I don't want to stuff Hal Winkler. I want to go home. I want to ask if there is any other way, but it's too late.

The knife digs into my gut and slides upward. Like one deep paper cut. I spill out. The lump disappears. This is it, I think. I should've done more with my life. I should've pushed my way to the front of that parade crowd as a boy. I should've taken out a loan and gotten that surgery. I should've gone to college. I should've visited Grammie in Assisted Living more often. I should've just stuffed Hal Winkler.

I should've, I should've, I should've.

Then it's over.

I'm hovering above Uncle Angelo as he fillets my carcass. He does what he does, knifing me artistically. My hide goes through various stretching and tanning machines. Eddie tosses all of my innards into a big furnace and brushes me with goop, laughing at my fingers that now look like deflated party balloons. He hangs me up to dry. Then they go upstairs. I stare at my flimsy self and frown at the remaining amount. I drift outside through the wall, avoiding pools of light made by the lamps in the taxidermy parking lot. I don't drift over handicap logos, because I grew up being told by Grammie that stepping on them was bad luck.

My ghost body isn't a body. From the chest down it's a series of thick pale threads, like I went halfway through a paper shredder. But my hands are the same knuckled lunkheads. I sit on a hydrant and wonder, What the heck now?

Another ghost appears with hands that look like fleshy oven mitts.

"Pop?" I ask.

"What was so wrong?" he says. "You think life is supposed to be easy?"

"I don't know," I say.

"You don't know a lot of things."

"Where's Ma?"

"Up there." Pop looks to the sky. "She figured it out."

"Figured what out?"

"Whatever it is you're supposed to before you can go up there. You better get figuring or this happens," he says and holds up his fingers, which have grown to the size of bowling pins. "Or worse," he adds, pointing to a ghost looking inside a mailbox.

"Purpose? You in there?" the ghost says, then reenacts hanging himself with one of his threads.

Pop turns back to me. "I got to go. I love you, son. I'm sorry you got my genes. I'm sorry for dying. I'm sorry for a lot of things. But I'm not sorry you're dead. You could've stuffed that guy. He was already gone." And he drags his hands away.

"Wait!" I cry. "Did your plane crash because you couldn't grip the controls?"

Pop frowns. "You've got some serious figuring to do," he says and drifts off.

What is left to figure out? I'm dead and still have these Sausage-Paws. And as I think this, I hear a stretching sound and my hands grow.

Ghosts wander on sidewalks, in cars, on rooftops, in tire swings. Some curse their murderer. Some stand outside their old bedroom, wailing as their widow makes love to a new person. Others apologize by trying to shout or write on walls. Some ask where their Purpose is. Everyone reenacts his or her death. Some are animals. I can tell the ones that came from Stuff-A-Bear, because a Magical Foam Organ will fall out of a belly gash. Everyone wanders until they figure it out. When they do, a chime sounds and they rocket upward.

So I drift around and try to figure it out.

I drift to Shâbner's house. His wife rubs her temples as she pays the bills. Shâbner sits on the couch with icepacks on his shins, watching TV. Marshall sleeps in his lap with an icepack on his foot. The phone rings. Shâbner answers. I hear Eddie's voice. Shâbner's bottom lip quivers. "How awful," he says. He runs a finger through Marshall's hair and mentions that Blind Chris also knows how to use the Umbilical Cord. I slap him, but my hand glides right through.

Blind Chris is home, folding paper cranes. I shout, try to knock over a water glass. But Blind Chris continues to fold, snarling with concentration. Headlights flash outside and a sea-foam Caddy parks. I can't watch. I apologize and drift away.

Hal Winkler lies in his bed and reenacts getting bludgeoned and filleted and stuffed.

In my trailer, my origami models are stomped all over the carpet. On the bed is the SelfBear I made when I first started at Stuff-A-Bear. I overstuffed the paws and kept them tucked in the pockets. I drift through my walls with violent speed, raging at how much I'm going to miss. I was only twenty-five. I never got to marry, be a father, have proper hands to play catch with my child. Make a toast. See Niagara Falls. But I still could've done those things. I could've driven to the falls. I could've asked out Emily at StickyBunz Bakery, maybe married her, toasted our love. I could've saved up and gotten that surgery, tossed a ball with our child. It occurs to me that I had no real Purpose in life. I was already twenty-five.

I sob. Moths flutter through my head and out of my mouth.

I reenact getting filleted and stuffed. My hands stretch and grow.

I drift through what the tornado didn't chew up of the cornfield, around the trailer park, over debris piles that used to be neighboring mobile homes, up and down the twisty slide thrown into someone's yard from the school across town, past the beatniks in lawn chairs chucking stones at geese. I drift through the gully cattails and dampen my threads in the meandering stream where deer mate in their injured fashion. A muscleman ghost with deer antlers licks a birch tree and says, "Them tastes like Purpose?" He bucks his camouflage threads and reenacts getting shot. I drift through the orchard near the lake, tangle around a limb until one of the workers picks a nearby apple, jostling me free, and away I go.

At the state park beach, orange turds float in the frothing surf. Teens by the abandoned lifeguard tower feed gulls Alka-Seltzers to see if they'll explode. A fisherman ghost out on the lake uses a thread like a fishing rod. The palisades tower behind him. At the bluff's high ledge, a ghost boy shivers. He pleads, "Not again! Please, not anymore!" He cannonballs into a phantom boat below. He spasms before floating back up to the cliff.

My Magical Foam Organs fall out and I cram them back in.

Back in town, I sit on the curb, thinking I might be drifting forever with these pale hippos attached to my wrists. My hands make that stretch sound and grow even more as a toddler ghost crawls by and reenacts electrocution by sticking a finger in a thread shaped like an outlet. Another ghost uses one of his threads shaped like a putter to try to knock a soda can into a curb drain. I hold one of my own threads and, without thinking about it, manipulate it into a hopping frog. Then I grab a different thread and close my eyes. I fold a whale. That exciting feeling rises in my whispery chest again, rattling the chain-link fence around my heart. The models are ugly but I don't care. I fold a unicorn, a rose, quit worrying about my Purpose, and fold and fold until a menagerie dangles from me: goats and cranes and a dragon that almost brings a passing ghost to tears.

"Teach me?" the ghost asks.

"Close your eyes," I tell her.

She does. I place one of my threads between her fingers, set my hands over hers, and guide. She scrunches her face in concentration. After, I stick my hands inside my body. She opens her eyes to see a pale translucent frog. She laughs and glows.

"Your fingers must be made of light!" she shouts. She reenacts her seizured overdose and then adds, "The imperfections are so beautiful! How that leg is shorter than that one, or how that one is hornless!" Others gather around. The female ghost asks how do I manage to fold in the suffering? How do I manage to get it so right? She wants to see my hands. "Let us see the omnipotent sculptors!" she pleads. I shake my head. I imagine a chant of *MarshmallowDukes!* It shouldn't be about what they look like, I want to tell her.

And I'm about to when she reaches in and grabs one of my wrists. As her arm enters me, I get a whiff of incense and hear the distant jingle of her mother's oversized earrings, like dinner triangles. She raises my hand. I cringe, waiting for the jeers. But it never happens. And as I look into their faces, I see the suffering in their cloudy eyes, the appreciation for each delicate flaw in the disfigured paper animals. My fingers are their tongues. Cuticled voices that give them something to cheer about. And I'm glad I didn't stuff Hal Winkler or get that surgery, because I would have lost that voice. So I milk the rare moment, puff out my chest, and raise my other hand as the ghost crowd floats higher and applauds.

Then there's a chime and I'm rocketing up up up.

And as the night rushes past me, I think I'm ready to go anywhere. I'm ready for my own parade.

Elvis the Pelvis

This morning my front maple is draped with toilet paper. Lyle clings to my leg, teething on his leash tethered to the upright piano. A lawn gnome hangs from a limb by something metal, bent like a noose. Maybe the local teenage gang S.I.V. did this? I recently saw those initials spray-painted vertically on a lamppost at the playground, a phallus carved into the teeter-totter with a misspelled curse veined across the shaft. I shielded Lyle's innocent eyes. Except how did the gang jettison the toilet paper over the highest branches? Nobody can throw that high. Not without a ladder. Only that schmuck Tony Duda could maybe ever do that.

In high school Duda was the stud varsity quarterback. I was the elite trombonist nobody. Duda triple-pump-faked Forrest Andover Central High's secondary during Homecoming while the band marched and performed the alma mater with cunning tenacity in glorified foil sombreros. We called ourselves the Upstate Space Racers, which added flatulent hipness. Duda and his linemen were versatile student athletes. We were swirlied, wedgied, wet willied, noogied, nut tapped, Indian burned, charley horsed, spitballed, and purple nurpled. Duda once pantsed me in the cafeteria and exposed my underwear portraying Elvis Presley's snarling mug. The briefs were on clearance. Money was tight in my family. My parents were loving and uneducated. I didn't have confident leg hair yet. I started wearing two belts to school.

But a botched play left Duda with a shattered kneecap. The only time I witnessed him mortal and adolescent was in gym after the cast came off his atrophied pale leg and he struck out in kickball. We all laughed and reveled. I still see him limping around, checking tire pressure at the Polish auto garage or smoking outside the Bowl-O-Drome with his flaccid ex-linemen, high-fiving, their class rings haughty and topaz under the neon beer signs. I've wanted to tell him off for years. But whenever I think about actually doing it, I impulsively clutch my pants. So instead I went to Cornell on scholarship and got a bachelors in music. Maybe I'll teach when things start looking up again, if they ever do. For now, I'm making ends meet: selling insurance, erecting laborious overtures on my sleek trombone in the Drums Along the Mohawk parade each summer, trying to seduce the anguish out of me, refuse the skivvied boy from my youth, and serenade my lovely Tess back from her far-off place.

Looking closer: it's a bent trombone slide that the lawn gnome is hanging from.

I take out the old high school yearbook and find the marching band photo. I locate Art Fowler, the pudgy tuba player. Last week someone left a rusty tuba on his porch with a dead skunk crammed inside. I locate Mike Terenzetti, the nervous snare drummer with a fear of clipping his fingernails. Two days ago he found a tapered drumstick pierced through one of his car tires. Now me with the trombone slide noose.

Part of me wonders if S.I.V. actually did this.

On the opposite page is the football team: the Mighty Sputniks of Upstate. The kicker discreetly flicks off the camera. Some thick-necked kid tweaks another thick-necked kid's nipple, and the thick-necked tight end behind them laughs. Duda stands in the center, flexing.

I look back at the marching band photo. There's my gangly frame. There's Ron Swift, the gothic cymbalist. And Nolan "The Nerdo"

Barker. His finger is up his nose to the knuckle! The photo is somehow fraudulent with Nolan, ruined. In the front row I catch Tess smiling her large braced teeth. I almost recall the scent of peppermint when the doorbell rings. I quickly shut the yearbook and bury it under a stack of magazines, let in Ms. Soboloski, my sweet, mothballed sitter. I get ready for work, hug Lyle, and blow Tess a kiss goodbye. She is the middle of five copper urns on the mantel, sandwiched between both pairs of our parents.

*   *   *

I work in a drafty cubicle soliciting cancer insurance over the phone. Today a prospective client asks if I have a soul. I respond, What does that have to do with protecting his savings from a malignant brain tumor for only ten pre-taxed dollars a week? He says it has everything to do with it. Then he calls me a Gaylord and hangs up. I think about what he said. Not about being a Gaylord. About having a soul. How do I know if I do?

The photo of Tess on my desk: Lyle in her round belly, a motherly rouge to her cheeks. Her teeth, white and straight. If I look close I can see parts of me stuck in there.

Tess was the metal-mouthed majorette. She flossed three times a day. I still recall the smell of peppermint on her fingertips. The touch of her eyelashes across my face, like promises. Later in life we shared the mutual pain of becoming adult orphans. My father was the last to go, discovered in his recliner, covered in sitcom light. His body went into the Kiln and came out looking like a pile of smoked cigarettes and ceramic shards.

The Kiln is what we used to call the crematorium. It was macabre hip. High school toughs played tonsil hockey and guzzled beer behind it. I heard that Duda lost his virginity back there to dance team captain Miranda Stevens. In gym she could put her legs behind her head and walk on her hands. My gym shorts were denim to avoid the embarrassment of popped boners. So were Coach Fitzpatrick's. He gave me an "A" even though I couldn't climb the rope. I couldn't climb the rope because of the boners. I think the "A" was for our mutual empathetic denim. I lost my virginity in a cinder-block dormitory with Tess under the covers, nervous-breathed, our unsure hands navigating like demagnetized compasses.

I have plans to spread the ashes. But I'm not there yet. I'm still trying to get used to the strange silence of my house. Make sense of it. The way things smell less and less feminine, peppermint. I never take off my wedding band. I still set her plate at dinner.

* * *

Once a week I pay Ms. Soboloski overtime so that I can congregate at the firehouse for noncompetitive Bingo with former band members like Art and Mike and the trumpet section: Sarah Shoe and Tanya Mantel. Duda once took Tanya up to The Spot. Kids partied in the woods and cliff-jumped into the lake until that boy fell and died. There was a damp couch back in there, lawn chairs, a beer cooler, and a plot of scorched bonfire dirt. Duda felt Tanya up and made her beg for it until his buddies fell from behind the trees laughing.

I don't see Thom Gaff, the flutist who runs the local hardware store. But Nolan Barker is here, wheezing in his volunteer firefighter helmet and Space Racer poser letter jacket. While we rehearsed, Nolan sat in the bleachers with his sousaphone, groping the brass instrument as if he were trying to negotiate a brassiere. I only participated in one swirlie in my life and it was Nolan's. I think Thom held Nolan upside down. I guarded the bathroom door. Art and Nick contributed various tauntings. Nolan gurgled romantically. We all felt important and empty in that pubescent way. Nolan's retainer accidentally got flushed. Our band teacher, Mr. Mangini, awarded him a varsity letter out of pity. Right now that letter is poorly sewn to Nolan's denim jacket, fraudulently complementing his topaz school ring just one finger over from his wedding band. Someone actually married him! Though no one has ever seen her. He never talks about her. They must've divorced before he moved back. Maybe she's imaginary. Maybe he got tired of the sham of his life and consummated her out of thin air.

We play and chat: B-4. O-28. G-17. Etc.

At one point Nolan interjects that maybe we should have a jam session for old times' sake. He points toward his sousaphone – dented and mangled with an almost instrumental scoliosis. As he turns to get it, I hit him in the back of the head with a rubber fireman's boot. He twists his ankle and stumbles. We all laugh. Nolan's face gets red and varicosed, and he howls through gritted teeth, slapping his thighs. His left eye does a twitchy thing.

After that we call it a night.

On the walk home, I imagine my foggy breath as escaping bits of soul. I remember Lyle's complicated birth – the doctor's long, jowly face in the antiseptic lighting, shaking his head, calling it. Tess's machine flatlining, monotone. Lyle squirming and wailing in my arms, minutes new. My torso, a breezy subway tunnel. Lyle has his mother's large eyes, my corncob-thread hair; Tess's parents remembered in his ears; my father's impatient tendencies in flared nostrils; my mother's dignity in a freckle on his cheek. Rest all their souls.

I hold my breath to save what is left of me as church bells clamor in the distance.

*   *   *

Next day I remember to buy electrical outlet safety covers because Lyle is rapidly outgrowing his bungee leash. I stop by Thom Gaff's hardware store but it's closed. Thom never misses work. He won the Perfect Attendance award every year in high school. A few roofers peek into the dark windows and shrug. I decide to swing by Thom's to make sure he's okay. His lawn is littered with flashing sirens and camera crews and gossipy neighbors. A cop yellow-tapes off the yard as a long black bag is carried out of the house. The bag isn't zipped shut entirely, because a silver flute is sticking straight up out of it.

*   *   *

Suspicious pry bar marks were found on Thom's back door. But no fingerprints. No evidence. No witnesses. Thom's cross-dressing housekeeper said Thom played his flute in his sleep. Maybe he was sleep-marching again and fell down the stairs. How he/she knew about Thom's nocturnal recitals wasn't elaborated on. He/she was a suspect but released because he/she had a house key and wouldn't need a pry bar to enter. He/she is the one who found Thom at the bottom of the staircase with his flute through his gut.

I decide to call in sick. I give Ms. Soboloski the day off and spend it with Lyle. I occupy our attention with shiny rattlers. I fly us around the living room like an airplane. He coos and giggles. I entertain us with soft melodies on my trombone, read us an insurance brochure to instigate nap time. I wipe Lyle's drool. I wipe my eyes. He yawns, flipping his wrists at the mobile above his crib. I yawn, flipping my wrist, turning pages of photo albums, accompanied by the nervous click of my furnace's electronic ignition.

The click of the Kiln's electronic ignition.

I think of Tess, her starry teeth. I make individual wishes.

And I think, Poor Thom Gaff. Poor innocent harmless genuine Gaff.

Who would do such a thing? Who could?

At dinner I set two plates. I wonder if I should put food on the other, hers. Maybe she's still in the shower, or working late tonight.

Maybe I'll drape one of her blouses over the chair. I tap my fingers on the table. Lyle imitates, slapping his palms on his highchair, bouncing Cheerios onto the floor. I pick them up, consider setting some dental floss by her water glass when I notice a topaz flash. I see a small circle of fog between two handprints on the windowpane. Outside, a shadowy figure hobbles away and jukes right, as if muscle-memoried, between some neighboring hedges and disappears.

*   *   *

At the next Bingo we burn a candle for Thom. Our voices echo around the firehouse, off the new post-tornado façade and laminated CPR instructions and boxy cherry-colored trucks with the tall, tall ladders. After one game Sarah lightly touches Thom's candle and runs out sobbing. She and Thom shared backyards as children, first sandbox kisses. Tanya has one runny mascaraed eye. She'd been too bereft to do up the other. We recall the times Thom won the Perfect Attendance award, that odd way he parted his hair, how he played his brand-new silver flute at graduation, improving us all with a solo rendition of the alma mater.

That silver flute sticking up out of the long black bag, like a smokestack trickling soul.

Nolan screeches, "*Bingo!*" and pumps his fist.

We're all Bingoed out after that.

But before we go, Nolan again suggests having a jam session and starts tenderly marching in place. He still knows the routines he never had to memorize. I recognize certain moves and long for the Astroturf under my choreographed feet, the warmth of the stadium lights on my peach-fuzzed upper lip, stealing glimpses of Tess and her reflective mouth as she maneuvered her baton with delicate balanced twirls, as if she twirled my heart.

Nolan taps my shoulder. He wheezes, struggling under the weight of his sousaphone. He smells like a medicinal lozenge.

"I think you should apologize for throwing that boot at me last week," he says. "That's not something you do to a fellow Space Racer."

"But you're not a Space Racer," I say.

He points to the varsity letter sewn to his denim jacket. I roll my eyes.

"I think you should apologize," he says again, setting down his sousaphone.

"Why is that?"

"We've both lost something," he says and fidgets with his wedding band.

Everybody is watching. It's so quiet I think I hear Thom's candle burning, or my own.

"Like you can share my pain?" I say, choked up.

Nothing has changed. We share nothing. Nothing, I tell myself.

"You're still Nolan the Nerdo," I say.

"And you're still Elvis the Pelvis!" he shrieks. His face gets red and varicosed again as he giggles and gyrates his hips, swinging his bent knees. He moves his outstretched arms and snarls his upper lip. That Graceland Lip. That Hound Dog Lip. That Jailhouse Rock Lip I've been refusing with my trombone overtures in the Drums Along the Mohawk parade that get progressively louder and more desperate. I hear Art and Nick catch themselves mid-chuckle. My wrist veins hurt. I tremble in a way I haven't before.

Nolan stops. When he grins, the lozenge in his mouth clacks against the back of his teeth. One eye does a twitchy thing. He picks up his sousaphone and I see it: the elastic band above his waistline. My knuckles whiten. I grab and yank.

Nolan yelps. Art's jaw drops. Tanya's eyes go wide. Nick puts a hand to his forehead, his uncut fingernails grinning like unlucky horseshoes. I grunt and go for the atomic finish. I want that waistband to cover his lozenge-clacking head.

I yank until that elastic band rips. That's when I let go.

*   *   *

On the walk home, sickles of frost begin to blemish the grass. Soul flits from my mouth, disappearing up into the purpled night. I ignore the almost turned feeling of my heart, convincing myself it's an okay and normal thing.

I pass the rival high school: the Fighting Muskellunge of FAC. Their band, the Anglers, was our biggest concern for four years. How things change. I consider heaving a rock through a classroom window to honor the good old days, but I just keep going, kicking a soda can past the Midnite Majestic Motel, filled with the cars of people who lost their homes in the tornado. I pass the KwikStop, Uncle Angelo's Taxidermy Villa, GrassBlasters Lawn Care, City Kritters Exotic Pets, and my office at New England Life & Mutual. I walk down the closed road of a neighborhood littered with storm damage, guiding myself by the pale carrots of light crossing in the sky at the distant minor league ballpark.

I pass the Bowl-O-Drome. Outside, mechanics huddle and smoke, hunched like strips of jerky with the last names Wrobel and Kowalczyk and Majewski, former linemen who found interesting geometries for stuffing me in my locker.

And Duda. He drags on a cigarette as the others high-five and belch.

One lumpy mechanic makes a stabbing motion with his hand.

Duda tosses his cigarette butt, and his high school topaz ring winks at me. The lumpy mechanic admiringly slaps his back.

No way no way no way, I think.

Then they disperse. I duck behind a parked car. I think I hear footsteps behind me, but there's just a scrap of paper tumbling. Duda hobbles behind the Bowl-O-Drome toward the thick stand of syca- mores and footbridge crossing the gully stream. Beyond that sits his trailer park, where beatniks mutilate geese and children wale on each other with dented Wiffle ball bats, crouching in the undergrowth and flickering cattails in wait.

I consider calling the cops. But the squad consists of old wres- tling jocks who Duda traded towel snaps with. They'd finger their cauliflowered ears and belly a chant of *Elvis the Pelvis!* before they pressed any charges.

It occurs to me that the world I live in is still one big popularity contest.

It's one big high school. One big Mighty Sputnik.

So I need proof. Evidence.

I put up my hoodie hood and tail Duda over the gully stream footbridge, through the sycamores, alongside the plot of chewed earth and rotten corn where the tornado touched down, and into the trailer park. Most trailers are dark and look like tuna fish cans. Others are bulldozed debris piles. Lampposts are bent perpendicular, and somebody has hung a tire swing from one. A man with cartoon- ishly large hands folds paper beside his open kitchen window. In the distance, a shirtless fink stands over a campfire and urinates on it.

Duda struggles up his porch and goes inside. I take a couple of hubcaps from the weeds and quietly stack them, climb to the window. Inside, a shadeless lamp raises a dead bulb, the ceiling fan is missing a blade. Nudey mags and beer cans cover the tops of stereo speakers. The floral wallpaper is yellowing. I search for an incriminating pry bar but don't see one. Then Duda limps in, his hands oily, muscles just enlarged ropes tied off at the ends of each bone. I spot a receding hairline. He switches on the television. An infomercial promotes a pedicure device, I think. It's hard to tell. The closed captioning is jumbled and wrong.

I keep low. My fingers start to numb and the overzealous crickets tattle. Undergrowth rustles behind me. But it's only the glow of a nearby bug zapper occasionally flickering blue. When I turn back, Duda is sitting with a beer and a plastic recorder.

He closes his eyes and places the instrument to his pursed lips. I hear its muffled and molested squawks. His fingers move awkwardly and incorrectly over the sound holes. His salt-and-peppered face implodes with each cracked pitch. On the television an audience member demonstrates the ease of peeling feet or pedicuring vegetables.

This time I think I hear a wheeze behind me. I turn. Nothing.

Then I hear one loud recorder shriek. I look. Duda is staring right at me.

The hubcaps topple and clank and down I go.

I get up and run. I hear Duda's front door swing open. At the sycamores I glance back and see a flashlight bobbing toward me. I run harder. My lungs ache, my arms push away branch after branch. I run so hard my hoodie hood flies off. I feel the cold air knifing right through my gangly frame. I'm pretty much all heart and bones and I wonder if that's all I've become. What the hell was I thinking? What am I doing out here?

As I cross the footbridge something hits the side of my face. Maybe a spiraling football? I trip. My head cracks into a stump.

* * *

Mud squishes beneath me. A leafy canopy sways above. A gap in the foliage bares stars and grumpy clouds that look like grandparents. My forehead stings and my gut gurgles a pukey kind of gurgle. I don't know where I am or how I got here. The last thing I remember clearly is flying Lyle around the living room like an airplane.

Then there are flashes.

Me, running. The hardware store closed. Lyle gnawing on his bungee leash. Nolan Barker yelping, "Bingo!" A lumpy mechanic making a vigorous stabbing motion. Thom Gaff with a flute in his gut. Duda playing a plastic recorder the color of bone.

A shadowy figure appears over me, huffing and puffing and wheezing. I want to ask for help, but I don't because I notice the pry bar. For some reason I recall Thom Gaff's cross-dressing housekeeper. The pry bar raises over the shadowy head.

"Wait!" I say, breathless. I think about the ashes on my mantel.

I want to spread my mother in the Oregon mountains of her childhood.

I want to spread my father in the Atlantic so he can travel the world.

I want to spread my in-laws over their family's hick Vermont farmland.

And I want to spread Tess, the love of my life, with me over the high school football Astroturf where we once marched. I want us spread in the end zone so that we can view the world from the perspective of someone who has triumphed.

A gentle rain thrums the leaves like one thousand fetal hearts beating.

"I have a son," I plead, "Lyle." I repeat his name: "Lyle, Lyle, Lyle."

The figure chuckles, the teeth clack. I déjà vu, whiffing medicinal lozenge.

I cover my face, cringing.

Then a beam of light catches the nearby trees, the pry bar. I notice a topaz glint on a finger and recall handprints on my windowpane. A flashlight bobs over the gully stream footbridge. By the time this other person limps up, the shadowy figure with the pry bar is gone, past the sycamores, juking into the Bowl-O-Drome alley.

* * *

This other person catches his breath and rubs his knee. Fat rain-drops interrupt the flashlight's beam with quick winks. I rub my face, sick from the slosh of watery mud beneath me. This figure wants to know what I was doing at his window.

"I don't remember," I say. There was someone else just now. Someone else with a pry bar. Maybe that was the person at his window? I thought I was going to die. Reunite with Tess too soon. Lose Lyle. My head burns. I ask if he's going to hurt me.

"No," he says. "But if this was years ago I'd have pounded you for sure."

The dry limbs of older trees moan and creak.

"You injured?" he asks.

"I think something hit me," I say, rubbing my head.

The flashlight investigates the surrounding woods. I rub my temples. I observe a cloud in the shape of a duck. A plane way way way up blinks a red light as it inches across the sky. The flashlight eventually illuminates a rubber fireman's boot.

I experience a familiar and almost turned feeling of my heart.

A tear arpeggios its way down my cheek.

"I want to go home to my son," I say. I think: Lyle, Lyle, Lyle.

The shadowy figure tells me I'm bleeding. He squats. It's Tony Duda. He removes an oily rag and presses it to my head, and the pressure feels nice so I don't protest.

"Can you stand?" he asks.

I try but the woods start to spin and my legs buckle. Duda catches me, sets me across his lap, and reapplies the rag. He says I might have a concussion. He's had enough to know the symptoms. I look into the deep hazel welts of his eyes and see a softness there that surprises me. I feel the stringiness of his muscles. A gust coils through the trees, and in this chilled drizzle I feel Duda shiver, hear him groan as he adjusts his bad leg underneath me, the screws in his kneecap. The alcohol on his foggy breath. I don't clutch my pants.

"Who was the someone else?" Duda asks.

"I don't remember."

"Why did they have a pry bar?"

"I don't remember."

"So what do you remember?"

"Things. Running. The sound of your recorder," I say.

"You picked a hell of a thing to remember," Duda chuckles. "I never played an instrument before. I just mess with it. A kid performed this flute concert thing at my high school graduation. It made me want to try something new like that. Musical."

Another breeze swirls around us. The hairs on my arms stand. As a child, I believed this meant lightning was about to strike. Duda hugs me closer. Our foggy breaths rise and compare suffering. Something scurries in the weeds. A frog belches obscenely.

"You just need to work on your breathing," I say.

"You play the recorder?"

"Trombone."

Birds cackle in the leaves. Duda pauses.

"Do I know you?" he asks.

"You once pantsed me in the cafeteria," I say. "I'm remembered for that."

The birds hush and eavesdrop.

Duda shakes his head, grimaces. "That was a long time ago."

Goose bumps rise on his stringy arms.

"It was," I say, and mean it. But I am still Elvis the Pelvis. Except that could mean anything: matured, determined from heartache, someone capable of forgiveness, a good father. But as I look at the fireman's boot, I think of Nolan Barker and see I'm still the Elvis the Pelvis involved with his swirlie years ago, his recent adult wedgie. I was his Duda. Still am. Nolan had too much faith in the kindness of others. That is why he practiced from the bleachers, learned the marches, kept coming to Bingo. I suffocated that faith. Like Duda had done to me. Now we share the fact that we don't share it. We've both lost something.

Would Tess be proud of this?

Pigeons could flock out of the breezy subway tunnel in my torso.

"People remember me too," Duda says. "I'm the guy who triple-pump-faked FAC's secondary," and he makes the violent stabbing motion of the lumpy mechanic. "Or I'm the guy who Hurts Dough-nuted him or called her fat and made her cry or stuffed him into a locker or pantsed you." Duda shakes his head. "But that's not really me."

"I'm so dizzy," I say. "This isn't me either."

We listen to the subtle percussion of the rain for a while.

"Listen," Duda says. "I've got an idea. How do you want to be re-membered? I'll remember you that way if you remember me the way I want to be remembered. What do you say? At least it's a start, right? Please, remember me –" and Duda trails off in thought.

How do I want to be remembered? When it's time to put me in the Kiln, I hope Lyle is happily married, maybe a father, a concert pianist. I hope my surviving band members, even Nolan, will light a candle for me at Bingo. I hope they will all speak of me as a man who did his best, fessed up and undid wrongs done, helped others when he could, an overall kind soul.

My heart trumpets for that possibility.

Then Duda decides. He asks me to please remember him when he was the subject of pettiness and cruelty. The moment when he felt like he really belonged. He asks me to please remember him as the boy in gym class who struck out in kickball.

And it's a start.

So I shut my eyes tight, and I do.

Not All the Dominoes Having Yet Fallen

The cornfield stretched along the road, and his brother disappeared into it. Dustin waited in the truck, yawning, fiddling with the radio, visualizing the final eighteen holes of the tournament, interjecting memories of work he and Shawn had once done for their father: varnishing crown molding and wainscot, mouths plasticky from polyurethane fumes, nostrils caked with mahogany dust – how Dustin missed his youth, the simplicity of being a boy – he and his brother pissing on piles of broken bricks behind the wood shop, backs turned, the wolf of adolescence clawing at them. Maybe something else was already clawing at Shawn? Wood stain emphasized the *M*'s of their palm lines. Or maybe they were *W*'s? Depends on how you look at it, Dustin thought. It could be something entirely different even though it was constructed the exact same way.

Dustin was giving up the hammer for the putter, or trying to. Shawn seemed to be giving up everything. And because of this, Dustin couldn't turn to enjoy the sunrise, the corn slanting and rustling, because it felt like a violation, a perversion. Shawn wouldn't even take his shirt off in public anymore. His voice altered in pitch and emphasis, something Dustin was embarrassed to joke and dub *sissified*. He'd have said it a year ago, before.

He reached into the backseat for a golf club, cold in his hands as he polished.

It happened after the tornado ripped through town. It came out of nowhere. "I feel trapped," Shawn cried. Dustin was rebuilding homes in the suburb leveled by the storm. He stood inside wooden skeletons; second-story toilets hung in the sky, suspended by plumbing. Cars wedged into the crotches of trees. Shawn sobbed, shuddered. It was amazing what the weather could displace. Terrifying what could change overnight.

"It's like claustrophobia, Dus!" Shawn said, grabbing Dustin's forearms as if to ensure he was paying attention. He was. Shawn accidentally scratched him. Dustin remembered when they'd fought as children. Their father always broke it up, curls of planed wood tangled in his forearm hair, reprimanding, *Boys don't pinch and scratch and slap.*

Now Dustin stood inside the new frames, squaring off their pine bones, knowing if it wasn't exact at the beginning, off even by a sixteenth of an inch, the structure would emerge so askew later that it would be almost impossible to cover the flaws.

Blackbirds released off of a scarecrow. The rustle of gold corn sounded like something hunting him. His caddy finished his squat, hiked up his skirt, adjusted the bra padded with the same gym socks he sometimes wore to racquetball, and trotted out, retying his hair into a ponytail. The stink of morning manure swelled in Dustin's mouth.

* * *

All Forrest Jr. knew about the fox was that it thought golf balls were bird eggs.

While seeding tee box divots or combing sand bunkers, a curse might ring out, and Forrest Jr. would look up just in time to see the beautiful red thing sprint into the trees, carrying a ball, avoiding the hurled seven iron that snagged in the bushes.

Sunrise, and Forrest Jr. chuckled thinking about it, the Croakies on the ends of his glasses jiggling. He'd laughed too loud once as the fox scampered away and a second golf club had whizzed by his skull and dented his mower. He rubbed his thumb into that dent now, waiting for the sprinkler system to rise from the fairways and spit – his favorite part of the day – clicking and whirring, creating small rainbows like ghosts of dead golf shots.

Weather was holding up all tournament. Just a few menacing-looking clouds, all bark and no bite. Greens were running fast according to his Stimpmeter. Bunkers needed vigorous raking, just agony on his rigid spine. Still, Forrest Andover Jr. took great pleasure in his work: determining where he might set the pins in the undulating greens; watching skilled golfers make magic with the slopes and slants and doglegs he primped; the lesser golfers humiliating themselves red off the Bermuda fringes into the Bahia roughs surrounding the bentgrass greens kept a felty and meticulous eighth of an inch.

He'd reseeded the tee boxes with creeping zoysia. The ball sat up like a guilt-stricken mutt just begging for the rolled-up newspaper.

For the tournament he'd ordered extra sod. Unreplaced divots were a major pet peeve. If those fools only knew what went into the surface they chunked up! If they would crouch down to the green for something other than reading the grain and pitch of their putts, they'd see the care, the life, of Forrest Andover Jr. in the level.

The fox had become another course hazard. If it stole a ball, the golfer had to drop a new one, costing a penalty stroke. He'd been trying to capture it all summer. Once, he camped off of fifteen near the eggplant-shaped bunker, sitting with his Smith & Wesson .22LR pistol, listening to the cicadas work their ratchets in the dark, dew collecting on his toes, catching lightning bugs in the empty mason jar he'd decanted a couple beers into.

Must be a burrow somewhere with maybe a hundred balls in it, he figured.

The sprinklers rose and rainbowed, but Forrest frowned, robbed of their joy today.

Punchy Phillips was making an appearance during the final round of the Upstate Open, plugging the reopening of Anabolix gym in the mall since last year's tornado. Punchy had been lightweight champion after the Second World War. *The Fastest Hands Alive,* a newspaper claimed. Now he was mid-shuck of an exoskeleton, bouting with Parkinsons. Punchy had been friends with Forrest Sr., whose hands hadn't been fast enough with a grenade in the trees of France, and Forrest Jr. sometimes sat on the mossy felled trunks deep off the course, the birds chirping, light flickering through the breaks in the leaves, dandelion spores floating through the limbs like old childhoods, his nose itching, eyes watering, wondering what it must have been like to die like that, to witness these very same things in that way.

Forrest Sr. had owned the local theater, his father's before him. Forrest Jr. was to be the heir. But Punchy bought it cheap off of Forrest's mother after returning from the war. She was weak with bone loss and grief. She bagged groceries. There was no life insurance, just a flag and minor military condolences. In school Forrest Jr. became terrified of hot potato.

Punchy turned the Andover Theater into a gym with a boxing ring.

"I had no idea, none," Forrest's mother said, tearing up. "No idea he'd *tear it down.*"

Old postcards could be found in thrift stores around Upstate. Sometimes one appeared with a flashing Andover Theater marquee in the background. Forrest Jr. bought them up. He would decipher the faded cursive on the back for any hint of his father. It was all dead history. The Bowl-O-Drome sat on that plot now. His family tree was forkless branches of Only Children. His mother, long passed. Forrest Jr. never married.

"The seats were upholstered with a fabric called Red Velvet Cake!" his mother would say. "People were always snoring. Even during matinees." She described the auditorium's decorative candelabra as an octopus on strings. "It looked like an iron marionette with candles as big as your arm!" She'd sweep her hands, describing the coffered ceiling, the stage built with recycled saplings killed off by Dutch Elm disease – how once during rehearsal a dancer screamed when a beetle crawled out of a knot in the wood. "And there's the balcony," she'd say, pointing to some photos Forrest Jr. found in the attic. "Chuck Poletti sat in that very balcony for *The Nutcracker*. But this was before he became governor."

Now his father stood at Forrest Andover Central High. The bronze statue pantomimed a hand-wound movie camera. His mother explained that Forrest Sr. would actually do this. *A moment to remember*, he'd say through his hands. Or, *I want to remember this.* "He did it the day you were born," she said, pinching Forrest Jr.'s chin.

Once a week Forrest Jr. stopped by the school and cleaned the bird droppings from his father. He scrubbed the large fingers and imagined them blown off by the grenade. Forrest Jr. had driven halfway to Canada during the Vietnam War, fearing the draft. What would this man have said? *That was very unAndover.* Maybe, maybe not. Depends on what he thought during those last moments in the trees. *This was a mistake, I shouldn't have come here.* Or, *This is the most important moment of my life. A moment to remember.* And maybe his father turned the camera – what was left to pantomime – on himself, to film the light go dark.

*   *   *

They circled the course four times. Ted's hands trembled. Those hands had been so steady in the ring, Ellie remembered, but not when he proposed. He'd faced men bigger and stronger without a glimmer of fear, taking them down in flashes. But how nervous he'd been in that park, on his knee, his hand shaking the ring up at her!

She cried for him harder now than when he'd returned from fights swollen and cut. These new wounds wouldn't heal. His head sometimes jerked. He slowed, grew stiff, his body stubborning. His muscle-memory forgot, eyes darting with milky recollection. His body was breaking down, open. All the vulnerabilities and weaknesses he'd hidden from the world in his strategy and arrogance were slipping through the cracks.

They were fifteen minutes late.

"An-noth-er lap," Ted said, his hands trembling. Ellie held them.

It was getting harder to hide. His voice shook the way it did if he were fighting tears. She'd noticed this kind of restraint years ago. Home from the hospital, Harvey had wailed all night. She felt Ted touch her so gently she couldn't believe his hands were capable of the violence people paid to see. He whispered, "Go back to sleep. I got this. You took care of him for nine months. Least I can do is get him for a while."

Harvey at six: grabbing his father's bicep, Ted lifting him clear off the ground.

Harvey at fifteen: his first school fight. Ted had fought in Atlantic City the night before. Both sat at the kitchen table sharing a bag of frozen peas. How horrible Ellie felt, a failure. Her two boys injured and only one frozen bag between them!

Harvey at twenty-one: Ellie kissing his patchy stubble at his college graduation. Both he and Ted couldn't grow beards. She had to go up on her toes, and he had to lean down what felt like an impossible distance, her son getting too far away from her.

Then Harvey's heart attack at thirty-eight.

"I thought a Valdez hook was bad," Ted's voice tremored. "A Patterson uppercut, Dyson's jab. I've pissed blood, fractured both eye sockets, collapsed a lung, had six concussions. But nothing has ever felt like this."

My champion, she thought, *this is what it feels like to lose.*

Harvey was buried in the family plot overlooking Upstate Lake and the palisades, where a child had once fallen, drowned, and disappeared. Harvey had been gone fifteen years, but the wound felt as fresh as the grave, yesterday yesterday yesterday, lowering him down there. She and Ted had just placed flowers beside brittle ones left by Harvey's wife, Shannon, and their grandson, whom they rarely saw anymore. They kept tabs on him by the letters left at the headstone, watching the handwriting mature. "Look," Ellie pointed out, "Andy's writing in cursive now. He doesn't know the difference between *your* and *you're.*" Ted leaned in and shuddered. It had been a cool morning but Ellie knew better. There were multiple unfairnesses in the world, and here were several at once: the grave, the grandson, the aging.

Inside the limo, her husband's head stopped jerking.

"O-kay," he said.

Ted founded Punch Out Parkinson's! At the turn, he would challenge golfers to a closest-to-the-pin contest on the practice green using a punch shot: a low trajectory strike to avoid branches. For every golfer who beat him, Ted would donate fifty dollars. He wore his Anabolix gym polo. Twenty-five percent of gym memberships went to charity.

"Are you sure you're ready?" Ellie asked.

Ted closed the distance between them and kissed her cheek.

* * *

Forrest Jr. stood at the back of the crowd as Punchy hobbled out of the limo.

His mother had kept a few dusty marquee bulbs on her mantel. She'd ferreted them from the demolished rubble. When the theater was built, she and Forrest Sr. made handprints in the wet cement somewhere. No doubt Forrest Sr. pantomimed the moment in film. No doubt the imprints were incorporated into a cornerstone. No doubt his father's handprint was the ghost of the one blown off by the Germans. Sometimes Forrest Jr. picked one of the bulbs off his mantel, held it like a baby bird, and maybe felt the warmth of old light.

Punchy mimicked a few jabs. The crowd cheered. Forrest Jr. adjusted his sunglasses.

If he offered one of those bulbs to Punchy, it would only shatter in his callused, clumsy hands! Apology? The boxer's powerful and blank eyes darting over all the faces admitted that he didn't surrender to such things as apology and forgiveness.

The newspapers maintained that Punchy had had an effective defense.

Forrest Jr. kept a shoebox of Punchy's newspaper clippings under his bed beside the shoebox of Andover Theater postcards.

He retreated into the woods, probably in very unAndover fashion. He sat on a stump. The warm muggy air weighed on his lungs. A butterfly rested on his knee then floated on. A few crickets chirped in the shade brush. *Punchy the Impenetrable,* a clipping's headline read.

A grunt echoed through the trees. The sound was like someone getting the wind knocked out of them with a sock to the gut. The mating call of the fox. It was molting season. Tufts of red fur snagged in the bushes. It had been dispatching the guttural bark all summer, and as usual, with great empathy from Forrest Jr., no grunt returned its request.

* * *

Shawn disappeared into the trees to pee. Dustin had seen him stand between the restrooms at diners and stores, looking back and forth. He knew which one he belonged in, but which would welcome him? Shawn had managed to isolate himself from the entire world, and Dustin couldn't fathom the loneliness that matched the pumps and purse.

"I'm Shannon now," Shawn said. "I've always been."

"So does that mean you like – ?" Dustin began. "I mean, as – ?"

"I'm not gay, Dus."

Shawn explained it wasn't about wanting different things. It was just the point of view of the wanting. His smooth jawline was blemished with calluses and the faint discolorations of scarring. He waxed his beard and picked at the ingrown hairs with tweezers. The calluses almost looked as if his masculinity were trying to resurface. Shawn mentioned a laser hair removal surgery that would remedy the problem forever, and it was the first time Dustin really considered the permanence of this, of anything.

"Surgery?" Dustin said. "What if you change your mind?"

"I won't."

"How can you make a claim like that?"

Shawn shrugged, "Because I know me."

Once, in private, Dustin wore lipstick that belonged to a girl who'd spent the night, and he sat in his recliner with a beer. The weight of it on his mouth, smudging the lip of the bottle. He tucked his genitals in front of the mirror but felt no different, save for a dose of embarrassment. It was the Y chromosome, he determined. It couldn't be extricated. The body wasn't a line of dominoes. You couldn't expect the genes and cells to play along.

He didn't want to think about where Shawn's share of the winnings would go. Every birdie, every fewer stroke, was a contribution to it. Now, with nine holes remaining in the tournament, Dustin was only three strokes back of the leader.

On workdays he entered Thom's Hardware and saw Shawn sweeping and stocking shelves in clothes that conformed to shapes his body wasn't supposed to have but was slowly acquiring with diet and exercise and estrogen pills. The way his hips moved, as if his body knew it. He somehow had insight into what most men wished to understand and, like a woman, Shawn wouldn't divulge an ounce. With his back turned, roofers and plumbers didn't know better. *The things I'd do to her. I'd like to ring her dinner triangle.* A white protective rage burned for his little brother. But a red humiliation also lingered, and a yellow shame when Shawn turned and the men saw the truth – not all the dominoes having yet fallen.

Shawn in elementary school: clip-on ties, the lunch pail designed like a briefcase.

"What do you want to be when you grow up?" people asked.

"A businessman," Shawn said.

Dustin never wanted to work construction or be a golfer. *Nobody turns out the way they say they're going to as children*, he thought.

Shawn trotted out of the trees. "There's a man on a stump back there," he said, crossing his legs. "I think he's crying."

Dustin shrugged and drove.

At the turn: the practice putting green, the large canopy and the old couple sitting beneath it, holding hands. Dustin knew who they were. Growing up, their father had watched all of Punchy's fights. Now he looked like the puppet of a former champ tossed into a corner. It was terrifying to think about what the body could do to itself.

Shawn jogged over to the old woman and complimented her dress.

Dustin and Punchy shook hands. The old man shivered.

"*Wom-en*," Punchy joked. "That your sister? See the res-emblance."

He glanced at Shawn. The old woman cringed, and so did Dustin. He nodded, sucked spit through his teeth, and took his shot: a low worm-burner that rolled off the back of the green. Punchy hunkered over his ball and pendulumed like an unclasped fence gate. His chip rolled up onto the fringe. A staff member measured the shots. Punchy won.

"Don't wo-rry about it," Punchy stuttered. "We're don-ating for ev-erybod-y."

Dustin reached into his wallet, removed a fifty.

"Fair is fair," he said. He shook Punchy's hand and returned to the cart.

Then he heard the old man say, "W-hat's your n-name?"

"Shannon," Shawn replied.

"Shann-on," Punchy repeated. "Pretty na-ame for a pretty g-girl."

Glancing at his brother in the cart, Dustin recognized the kindred blush running down Shawn's throat. But, in the feminine cut of Shawn's polo, Dustin saw how the color spread across his clavicle, down his triceps. And in the skirt, how the blush swept over Shawn's thighs.

The tenth green was hidden around the tree line, a dogleg left.

"Work the draw," Shawn suggested, handing Dustin the driver.

When Shawn had pissed on the piles of bricks behind the wood shop, his underwear had showed, the top of his butt crack winking. Men let those intimacies hang out like hems of their dress shirts. But now if you saw something like that on Shawn, Dustin thought, it meant it was a privilege, and you had somehow earned the right.

Dustin tried the draw, but sliced.

The brothers watched the ball turn right instead of left, out of bounds.

* * *

Ted's body controlled his swing, allowing only segments to function. Golf revealed age and weakness. Ellie sipped water from a conical paper cup and fanned her face as Ted's secrets were publicized. The grinding of the bone in his right shoulder socket, the cartilage worn down from repetitious jabs and hooks. His eyes bulged pleas at the club as it involuntarily jumped in his hands like a leashed bloodhound trying to go after its hunt.

Some of the golfers mentioned that their fathers were Ted's former classmates. Others had known Harvey, reminiscing about sleepovers and birthday parties. Ted feigned nostalgia. Dementia was setting in. Memories were tipping over one at a time.

He was showing less emotion now than when he'd been champ. But what if he wasn't *showing* less, but *feeling* less? The pretty girl who was caddying for her brother had the same name as Harvey's wife. Ted didn't even flinch.

Ellie nearly collapsed under the weight of heartache. Recollection could be such a crime. The idea that time healed all wounds enraged her. What if she didn't want to be healed? What if she never wanted to lose that grief? Because what would it mean if she did?

And what if Ted was losing all the good memories? Or worse, what if he was losing all the tragedies? What if the pain was lifting as his mind scoured itself? The day she took him to the lakeside grave, the day he didn't quake for the right reasons, the day he tilted his head on his own with confusion, would be the day she'd want to die.

*   *   *

Three holes later, Dustin was six strokes back of the leader.

He looked at his ball and felt no urgency to punish it. He understood that when a golfer's confidence tumbled, it was only a matter of time before the rest of the game toppled with it. The putter weighed in his hands like a hammer. He drew his club back and thought, *Choke, duff, shank.* His drive off thirteen skidded into the tree brush.

Birds tweeted, spectators sneezed, balls driven from distant tee boxes clinked like toasts, leaves whispered, acorns fell and rustled in the dry growth. And then there was the *snap* of a makeup case, the *brushing* of hair, the *pucker* that welcomed lipstick.

Approaching the weeds where his shot had landed, he saw a red tail fidget and disappear.

He and Shawn searched for the allotted time.

Then Dustin dropped a new ball.

* * *

Forrest Jr. drove around the course on his mower, delivering seed and sod to his crew who repaired the par three tee box divots. Once, a curse rang out and Forrest Jr. expected to see the fox, but instead a golfer slammed his club down. Forrest Jr. winced for his fairway, for the golfer. It was always hard to witness a meltdown, a failure of the body, the mind.

On his walkie-talkie a crew member requested a large order of sod at the practice green. "Grasshoppers got nothing to hop to," the crewman relayed. "The mantis has lost his camo. The earthworm is naked. Major deforestation. Over."

They met at the maintenance shed. "It's that punch shot contest," the crewman said.

Forrest Jr. imagined the divots, the grass hunks piled like bricks, the rubble of his hard work. In the shed he kicked over a stack of seed. It spilled in whispers. Behind the stack he found the tent, the mason jar of dead insects, the Smith & Wesson .22LR pistol. He blinked at the gun then quickly hefted a roll of sod out to the crewman's trailer, saluted him as he drove off. A grunt echoed through the trees behind him. He unclenched his fists and looked at them – they'd begun to claw and mangle from years of raking and weed-pulling. His skin was raisined and unfit. Nobody would ever love him now, he thought.

Inside the shed he took the pistol and tucked it into his khakis.

He marched into the woods until the spectators' applause became hushed. He leaned against a tree with sweating bark and inhaled sweet pinesap. He blew his nose into his pocket kerchief, pollen thick in the air. He took the gun out and put it to his head, then down to his side, back to his head, then down again. Then he lay on his back and pulled his sleeve over his right hand. He shut his eyes and held his breath as long as he could until he saw stars. He tried to think about what it was he was thinking about in that moment, his body craving air, believing he was close to death, the closest thing he'd been to in a very long time.

Forrest Jr. sat up and gasped, lightheaded.

He stayed down until the tunnel vision passed and the sun and quiet opened up to him again, returning the defeat in his heart. Standing, he dusted his pants and walked, trying to navigate toward the sounds of the tournament.

The trees broke and Forrest Jr. stumbled into the parking lot.

A driver smoked on the hood of a limo, trumpeting his cigarette. His long brown fingers built for plotting piano octaves, the keys and chords callused on his fingertips. Forrest Jr. figured him for a jazz musician or at least a devoted hobbyist. If you took a picture of him, you'd see Chicago, St. Louis, red-light district reflections in his eyes.

"Hot one," the driver said.

Forrest Jr. dabbed his face with the kerchief. The driver wore an Anabolix button. Bird droppings dried on the windshield. He thought of his father's statue, the grenade, the course, and squinted into the sun. "Could use a break," he said.

"Not going to let up," the driver said, exhaling smoke through his nostrils.

Forrest Jr. blinked.

"Heat index won't peak till Thursday, says the meteor man," the driver said, offering a cigarette. Forrest Jr. had smoked only a handful in his entire life, the last being at his mother's funeral. But something threatening spiked the air, maybe the uric acid in the bird droppings that scarred light brown patches on his fairways, something that made him mourn what had yet to happen, his own capacity for destruction. He took the cigarette and lit it.

"Tobias," the driver said.

"Forrest," he coughed in response. Tobias smiled.

"A cherry-lunger," he said. Then he nodded at the wand hooked to Forrest Jr.'s belt. "You some sort of security or meter man, Forrest? I ain't parked illegally, am I? Got the handicap tag on the rearview," and he tapped the windshield with a knuckle.

Forrest Jr. looked at the Stimpmeter on his belt.

"No. This is for reading green speed. I'm –" He paused. He stared at the Anabolix button: the silhouette of a flexing muscular man that formed the *A*; the tiny fists touching to make the bar that connected the man's/letter's legs. "I'm the turf pro," he said, feeling the heat of the sun, the anger and shame in his heart, unAndovering all over the place.

Tobias wiped his forehead and dropped the ash from his cigarette by tapping it on the side mirror. "Bet it's nice to get sunshine and fresh air. I'm stuck in this elegant cow all day chauffeuring people around like I got nothing better to do."

Smoke burned and whistled out Forrest Jr.'s large nostrils. "Got to be nice to get air conditioning and shade," he replied, dabbing his upper lip.

The driver laughed. "Ha! Walk in my shoes for an hour, pal. Trust me, the AC ain't worth it."

Forrest Jr. scratched his face and took a long thoughtful drag. "Okay," he said.

*   *   *

If Dustin could have his way, he'd let bygones be bygones, bodies be bodies. He envied his parents' ability to walk the circumference of the situation. Their mother bought neutral gift certificates to the mall department store. Their father just played up an onsetting deafness from a lifetime of whining saw blades and hammering.

The crowd was growing around his implode. He was only a nine iron away from the eighteenth green, escape. At home he would shrink into his recliner, sulk in his underwear, and watch a *Cops* marathon while drinking himself into a decent torpor. He could look at those blurred faces on television and be goddamn jealous of them.

Or he might set his clubs at the curb on trash day, return to the job site, ice his shoulder after a long day of hammering. That was a choice, too.

Dustin took practice swings.

Shawn plucked some grass and tossed it. The wind pushed them right.

Someone in the crowd muttered, "The caddy's wearing briefs!"

Someone responded, "I seen them tighty whities! And there was a *bulge!*"

An official held up his QUIET PLEASE sign.

Shawn clasped his hands in front of him and gravity pulled the blush down again.

Dustin felt an untethering, a toppling. It blemished his face, he narrowed his eyes.

"Dustin," Shawn said in a low, old voice. "Do something."

"Golf is a game of minding your own fucking business, *Shawn*," he hissed, and turned away. He took his shot. The ball leapt like a wild elk, an elegant burst from the divot he sculpted in the turf. It landed with a faint *tuft*, dead center of the green.

But there was no cheer for the shot.

Shawn was gone. The crowd had parted and all of their heads were turned to the trees.

*   *   *

The limo took a different route to the hotel, Ellie noticed. Maybe a construction detour? She saw an orange-vested municipal worker marking a telephone pole with spray paint, indicating where the sewer line needed repairing, drawing an *S* and a downward-pointing arrow. They passed a strip mall of Uncle Angelo's Taxidermy Villa, GrassBlasters Lawn Care, City Kritters Exotic Pets, and an office for New England Life & Mutual. The KwikStop was still there and the firehouse had been renovated with a stone façade after the twister. "That's new," Ellie said. They passed storm damage, foundations of homes, stumps in yards, children hopscotching. *How things change,* she thought.

The limo slowed past the Bowl-O-Drome. The driver knew, too. This had once been Ted's first gym. He'd built it with his own two hands, his *bludgeoners,* as he called them, kissing his knuckles during prefight weigh-ins. But he and Ellie hadn't yet met then. First he had to step in a puddle, autumns later, crossing Genesee Street, and splash her dress. He had to offer to pay the dry cleaning, drop it off. She still had to invite him in for tea, play "Heart and Soul" together on her grandmother's baby grand. It was the only thing he knew how to play. Everyone knew how to play it, she thought, but she already liked him enough not to tell him. He had room for improvement. She watched his thick, clumsy fingers hit the keys, not familiar with minute precisions and graces. He still had to learn them, her.

"Look, Ted," she said, and turned.

Her husband's eyelids struggled to stay open. His head lolled. Small red lines wrinkled his nape where she'd missed with suntan lotion.

* * *

He found his brother about a hundred yards into the trees, a short par three away.

Shawn had his back to him. If Dustin hadn't known who was standing there, if he'd been just another roofer or plumber shopping in Thom's Hardware, he'd have thought the woman peeking around that tree might be beautiful.

His brother turned, his lashes clumped with mascara, and placed a finger to his lips.

Like childhood hide-and-seek. Finding him in his clip-on tie, squatting under the table.

Dustin carefully moved forward.

Beyond them stood a large blackened oak that had been struck by lightning, tipped into the crotch of another tree. Bright lime moss and dandelions scaled the trunk. The roots were pulled up and suspended in the air like a cluster of inverted ballerinas, exposing a burrow beneath. In front of it, a large red fox napped with its head on its paws. Around the tree, several kits wrestled among at least one thousand golf balls.

"Do you see?" Shawn whispered.

But it wasn't until the fox got up to pee that Dustin understood. It had a thing between its legs. The kits chewed the golf balls, but when they got tired of the Callaways and Titleists and Pinnacles, they poked at the male fox's belly until it submitted, rolled on its side, and snorted, allowing the kits to nose where nipples would be on his mate. The red fox had the same black eyes as any fox Dustin had ever seen in pictures or films.

Then the fox picked up the babies by the neck scruff and took them into the burrow.

Dustin felt the presence, the body beside him. He shut his eyes and felt the grooves of his palms, the *M*'s or *W*'s, and recalled the time Shawn accidentally broke the vase that their mother inherited from Gramama. Shawn had peed himself and something softened inside Dustin, cementing in that moment. Their mother came home and wept and raged, trying to fit the ceramic shards together. And Dustin found himself telling her it was his fault, he'd knocked it over. He took the belt, the scold. Shawn stood, wide-eyed.

"Why?" Shawn asked him later.

Because he was who he was. They were who they were, was why.

And what had really changed since then? Dustin exhaled, opening his eyes, knowing that they were brothers, but it was a right that needed to be continuously earned, and when push came to shove, he'd do anything he could on this earth for her.

*   *   *

The limo stopped and Forrest Jr. paid the driver the extra twenty. The edges of the parking lot undulated with heat. Birds hovered and Forrest Jr. cursed them and their vandal incontinence. Flies buzzed up his fat nose and he swatted them away.

He opened the back door. The old man was asleep. His wife looked confused.

"What's going on? Where is the hotel?" she asked.

"Quick stop, Miss," Forrest Jr. said. "Part of the Anabolix promotional tour."

The limo smelled like some balm. Forrest Jr. breathed through his mouth.

Punchy woke with a snort, blinking, jerking his head around like a chicken. His arms were freckled sausage casings with fists. Forrest Jr. saw old victories in the calluses, the forgings of things undone, broken down, unAndovered.

But the man's trembling made Forrest Jr. look away.

"Meeting with an old investor," Forrest Jr. said, scratching his palms.

"Honey?" Punchy's wife said, touching her husband's arm. "You never mentioned anything about another stop? Who are you meeting?"

Punchy looked up, a mute matte to his eyes. They moved in a way that said, *Questions questions questions.* He cleared his throat.

"Right. It's just a quick stop, hon-ey," he said. "Be right back."

The old man hobbled out. Forrest Jr. slowed his pace as they walked over to the big bronze statue, stopping in its lengthening shadow.

"What is th-this?" Punchy said.

"This is Forrest Andover."

Punchy jerked his head to the side and squinted.

"He owned a theater," Forrest Jr. said. His throat burned when he swallowed.

"Forrest Andover," Punchy said, "For-rest An-do-ver."

"You tore down the theater," Forrest Jr. said.

"I did?" Punchy said.

Forrest Jr. moved a hand to his back, felt the gun, and squeezed the handle.

"You came back from the war, and Forrest Andover did not," he said.

"I did?" Punchy said. "He didn't? For-rest An-do-ver?"

Punchy's eyes widened. "You're Forrest's little loaf. I sang you to sleep before the war."

Forrest Jr.'s grip loosened. In his periphery, his father filmed them, bird droppings on the hands pantomiming the camera. *A moment to remember*, he thought. He squeezed the handle of the pistol again. His throat tickled, his eyes watered. Best to let the fox go, he decided. There is already too much friction in the world.

He could do it right now. People would remember the name *Andover* forever.

"My mother used to say you were like a second father," he heard himself say.

"I was a father once." Punchy's voice wavered.

Forrest Jr. bit his lip. He wondered if he should shoot the fingers off the right hand of the statue, too. He wondered if he should just turn it on himself and unAndover. To split atoms, create more absence. His pointer finger slid over the trigger.

"Harvey?" Punchy asked.

"I'm going to kill you now," Forrest Jr. said.

*   *   *

Ellie watched it happen from the limo. What was left of Ted's soft and receded muscles tensed and flexed. His feet shuffled backward, then forward, reminding her of the way he danced in the ring: the stick and move. He'd had such elusive footwork. His hands lifted to his face. It was almost as if his muscle-memory was re-remembering. She dabbed her eyes. Things would get tougher. Ted was falling over, apart. But there was still some time, some fight. The man standing with Ted was about the age Harvey ought to be.

Ted knew it. She saw it.

The man reached to his back. Ted shuddered, extended a fist. Like how he feinted punches to get his opponent to open up and expose himself. His two bludgeoners would make ground chuck of the contending faces that peek-a-booed between the gloves, topple them all. He'd glow under the flashes, arms up in triumph. Now she watched as her husband unclenched that fist and placed his hand on the crying man's shoulder.

That Which Has No Fixed Order

only me and Momma's boyfriend Peat on the Peckinpaugh stage now, holding, holding, holding, that motherfucker him like a pecked scarecrow, me like a parade balloon leaking helium, cheeks puffed, soaked with sweat, all the disqualified contestants sitting with heads in their laps, except the guy who just dropped on his blue face, and now the medics are fanning him and sticking sniffing salts up his nostrils until he sits up blinking and gasping, a feeling very familiar to me as I reswallow the air in my squeezed lungs, my chest burning as the seconds collect on the judge's pocket watch engraved *To my Dandelion*, his white beard and bone frame like the dead weed, and as soon as Peat quits and exhales huge the judge will burst apart and carry across the stage smeared with berries from the pie eaters, soggy kernels in the plank gaps from the cob eaters, the CanalFest crowd cheering, chewing corn dogs and fried pickles, wearing foam mustaches of blond beer as they walk around watching Betsy Ross stitch her flag, the blacksmith pound shoes for the barge mules, the Drums Along the Mohawk parade, the eighteen-sixties church, the canal lock's north gate hydraulics booth, the Antique Barge Pavilion where the judge announces me and Peat have been holding for six hundred seconds, over halfway to the world record of one thousand one hundred and sixty-one seconds held by a free diver with lungs like Egyptian tombs, and me with the chronic apnea secret weapon, my lungs used to the lacking, me six when Momma couldn't wake me for fifteen minutes, sitting on a large toy pile, crying to God not to take me also, rubbing my head and stomach like she did to Pop when he got skinny, stocking up on blankets, telling me she still had a hard time telling me, I was her fragile button, her bruised fruit, she opened herself to make me, a pain I can't know and only imagine like the kidney stones years back, like someone reached up into me and struck the lighter's flint, a feverish ache and puke until I passed them and collapsed in the bathtub weeping, but this is not pushing something out to be proud of, all I can do is hold it in, hold it up to Pop's expectation, *You're going to be man of the house soon*, coughing, the smell of iodine clinging to him like sulfur in the well water, so I'm trying to win the Iron Lung trophy and add it to the lot beside Momma's golf clubs, buckets and vases and plastic food containers filled with tees and Titleists, trash bags of knickers and khakis in the sizes Pop wore as he thinned, wicker baskets, the cigar boxes or stacks of empty cigar boxes or cigar boxes full of matchbooks, mounds of miscellaneous along the hallway, dozens of blankets and pillows in two tight plots where me and Momma sleep, a photo of Pop tucked under one of hers, telling me *Hold on to everything, Bernie* when I come home from clerking at the KwikStop or drive her to Doctor Morgan or to the Social Security office to pick up a disability check, parking in the driveway, the garage gill-packed with plastic bottles, sewing machines and dress forms, fabric samples, carpet samples, shoe boxes of playing cards, the one rocking horse and so much else that blurs into one accumulation I call her "museum" because she likes to move through the narrow paths and tell me where and when she got stuff, a television wedged in each room playing home movies from the VHS bins of our family and families purchased at thrift stores and yard sales, extra VCRs stored in the broken fridge behind a tower of folding chairs that Peat claims is dangerous, that twiggy motherfucker got her laughing, his hand already on her hip when I returned from parking the car, next in the disability check line, leaning on her cane more in his direction than to the right like normal, and now Peat is purpling but still holding, a former navy diver, but who does he think he is? what does he think he's going to replace? I see some white flashes as the judge announces eight hundred seconds of holding, and I'm going to show Peat that holding is something we Gadwaws take for serious, we just don't get rid of things, and I know he's got it in his head he wants me gone with the rest of her museum, my record collection, the baseball gloves me and Pop wrapped in rubber bands, the hundred golf and hunting mugs filled with poker chips left at the foot of the propane grill on the porch, candles melted down to nubs, wax dripping through the cooking grate, all of it Peat wants to hire a truck and just dump, Momma already having slowed her curating since he came around, but no holy way in hell I'm forfeiting, and maybe the white spots are the crowd taking pictures as we approach the nine hundred second mark, a tight heat in my chest rising up my throat, pulling the strings behind my eyes, Peat on his knees and knuckles, the crowd roaring in and out, and I see Momma among them, sitting in her chair because she can't stand for as long as I can hold, and she's crying, spit strings in her open mouth, not liking this, me bringing it all back, but it was Momma who said after we buried Pop that no matter what we needed to hold our heads up high, so I am, numb on the same side my mouth droops toward until I'm tipping down down down in that direction, white spots fireworking, Momma younger and prettier before I got fat and Pop got sick, because I see kitchen countertops and the microwave and magnets on the fridge door holding a report card, she's wearing her wedding ring on the hand holding a lobster over a steaming pot, its eyes twisting, claws shackled, and I tell her *Don't,* but she says lobsters can't feel hot water like we can, *Look,* she says and rubs its head and stomach and the lobster calms, *It's hypnosis,* she tells me, *Fear alters the flavor of the meat,* and I remember this being when things started to change, Pop's first wheezes and shunts and yellowing, my metabolism slowing, and Momma held on, but the longer you hold the lobster the longer it's afraid, and if rubbing calms it then the lobster must feel you, Momma, so how can it not feel the water? but I didn't have the lungs for such a thing then, just a boy who'd come in from a catch with his out-of-breath Pop, learning the slider and curve and change-up, and what I did was turn from the sizzle as she dropped it in and covered the pot with a lid

Everything in Relation to Everything Else

Television lights move over Sammy's face in a way he can feel. Maybe this indicates emotional depth? Later, Delilah will tie his hands with scrunchies, ride him belligerent in her Honda, then drop him off. Sammy imagines the impending ache and bruises, turning his old high school football championship ring. The MVP engraving is his cross to bear. But he tells himself this is safer, this Delilah fiasco. It's better than nothing.

Then a commercial: two bikinied babes on horseback blow cartoon kisses in slowmo. Here are local singles waiting to chat! These lights feel exclusive to Sammy. He navigates Kiss&Tell.com®, creating a profile by uploading his picture and selecting three self-descriptors from the site's database that will match him with other compatible users.

Here is a user already clicking Sammy's Pinch LoveButton™. She types via Insta-Flirt™ that she won't go on a SimuDate™ with him until they get better acquainted. Sammy couldn't agree more, thrice divorced. Soon his children will return from their respective mothers and compare notes, looking for themes to connect the failed marriages. They'll sometimes chaff him, calling him Rent-a-Mom. Sammy can take a joke, laughing hard enough that when the tears come they'll be inconspicuous. Miranda315's profile picture shows a brunette holding two young children. Her status: *divorcee*. Sammy Insta-Flirts™, How would she like to get better acquainted? She recommends the 20Q FactFinder™ app. Sammy purchases the app, figuring it's cheaper than a fourth alimony. He clicks Miranda315's Pinch LoveButton™, thinking his children are going to need a new nickname for him.

*   *   *

In his basement Canteen deletes spam email recommending solutions for the inadequate size and performance of his chubby. Where does the spam come from? The last witness to a chubby was the woman who played Betsy Ross at the Erie Canal Village. She'd been high school elite, the immaculate prom queen of Forrest Andover Central. He'd been a JV wrestler, nicknamed Canteen for his barrel-torsoed water retention. Here is how mortgaging facelifts and shepherding kids have felled Betsy Ross from her ivy pedestal into the Erie Canal lock's unoccupied North Gate Hydraulics booth, where she took a cigarette and Canteen's knuckles between her lips. She raked her nails across Canteen's back and called him Old Glory, and he felt like it. Did Betsy Ross even have his email? He rocks in his chair. Maybe the spam came from Mindy. Did she want him robust for her long-awaited return?

Just in case the spam is from Mindy, Canteen undeletes the message. He takes another swig of rum in the canteen sashed around his torso. The canteen is desert camouflage and wrapped with duct tape. The spam reappears. Deleting could be viewed as coming to terms. But so could undeleting. Undeleting, he thinks, could be moving on.

Canteen redeletes the spam.

The silence of the house. Canteen tries to will the floor above him to thump with footsteps across the now empty space, everything sold. The stubbed toes, the pubescent squawks. The door that won't slap shut again, the basement window that won't clink and chip with driveway gravel sprayed from gassed tires, the stovetop missing the odor of forgotten charring food, the smoke detector's beep that would go unrehearsed.

His real estate agent took care of the house. An inspector checked the foundation and confirmed the pipes weren't PVC. Canteen hadn't known if the foundation was T-shaped or slab-on-grade, but he knew the pipes weren't PVC.

Here is the drop ceiling panel above the dryer pushed aside. Here is the noose hanging down from a sturdy galvanized pipe.

The note beside the computer requests he be buried with both Fender Telecasters. Canteen bought TJ his own for his ninth birthday. By his tenth, he was strumming Straw Fogel's "Dixie Trixie" while Canteen mourned a beer bottle slid along his own strings. Canteen played that song into Mindy's gut. Then she never came home from the hospital. Movers came for her things. Last he heard she was in a Texas sanitarium trying to breastfeed a radio.

That had been twenty years ago.

The Telecasters' strings are brown with tarnish. He runs his hand over them.

But maybe Mindy will still come back. Canteen leaves the front door unlocked, just in case. Maybe she'll ask him to forgive her. Maybe she'll ask to see her grown baby boy, and Canteen will take her to his American-flagged plot.

Just in case Mindy returns, Canteen re-undeletes the spam. It appears beside a new email. The subject: *Miranda315 Has Just "Humped" You!*

The email reads: *Miranda315 has just clicked your Hump LoveButton™! Reciprocate now! Suave? "Wink" at Miranda315! Flirty? "Pinch" Miranda315! Why be alone? Try a 30-second video session with the Virtual Cupid™ app! You deserve it! Just think: how can you connect if you can't literally connect?*

He can't remember the last time he surfed Kiss&Tell.com®. Definitely not since the personnel officer and chaplain stood at his door holding the canteen and a flag folded into a triangle. Canteen recalls what the officer said on that damp morning: *It's easier to leave than to be left.* But Canteen knows it's not. He couldn't leave somebody. How could he when he knew so well how it felt to be left? Here is the kitchen sink in his gut, nobody left to leave.

Or is there? A chord forms on his heartstrings. Miranda315's profile: a blonde in an Upstate CC hoodie. Her descriptors: *Pianist, Perky, Gullible.* Maybe she knows the right fugue to his heart, how to harmonize with the complicated parts? He reviews his profile descriptors: *Musical, Attentive, Well in Doubt.* The last descriptor doubled as a crude joke about the girth of his chubby. Nobody ever got it. Mindy would have. She liked the subtleties of life, Canteen being one of them. Maybe he put the joke there to lure her back. Maybe she also traversed the fields of "New York's #1 SimuDate™ Service?"

Canteen swishes the rum in his mouth. He'd joined Kiss&Tell. com® for TJ. Once, all the Boy Scout troop mothers helped their sons earn basketry merit badges and Canteen showed up with a basketball and whistle. Another scout mother helped TJ weave his wicker while Canteen stood against the wall, blushed, cradling the ball.

Canteen fingers the sash around him decorated with fraying scout badges.

But how can anything be gained beyond what has already been lost? Maybe Miranda315 got his crude joke. Maybe Miranda315 got the joke because she knows Mindy. Maybe the spam really is from Mindy then? Maybe a world that has taken so much from him, singled him out for sacrifice, has decided to give something back. Canteen takes another swig, looking at the noose reflected in the computer screen like Straw Fogel's posthumous lasso reeling him in to a duet of "Dixie Trixie." Then he focuses on the variety of LoveButtons™

flickering onscreen, unclicked. He scratches his cauliflowered ears, certainly well in doubt.

* * *

Sammy on the phone:

"Hey, kiddo. Just checking in."

"Hey, Dad! How's your day off?"

"Oh, you know. Busy, busy, busy. You having a good time at your mom's?"

"Yeah, Joe showed us how to make English muffin pizzas."

"How'd he do that?"

"Put sauce and cheese on English muffins and then cook them in the toaster oven."

"Sounds like Joe is a real nice guy."

"Yeah, I think Mom really likes him."

"We can make those pizzas here, too, you know, whenever you like."

A pause.

"But then what would Joe do, Dad?"

* * *

Nabeet meditates in a locker room stall at Anabolix gym, sucking his yellow fingertips. He'd been right here when the tornado struck last year. Barbells shattered mirrors, treadmills stacked a dozen tall, and a parking lot dumpster dropped into one of the offices. One bench remained with a man still doing reps, muttering in shock. It happened so fast he hadn't even finished his set. Nabeet perspires harder, remembering: drip, drip, drip.

Tamara had crawled out from under her desk, papers strewn. He saw how the fear had pulled the blood into her face, and he loved her then. Nabeet faked a limp, said a five-pound plate had struck him. He told her he heard a clicking in his knee even when she didn't, her ear to it. God! "I have chronic tendonitis," he told her. "I think the storm's change in pressure re-aggravated it." She pressed and squeezed different places up and down his leg. She asked, Did this hurt, did that? He shook his head no, and fought the urge to touch her hand.

"Tendonitis?" she said. "I thought it was a five-pound plate? I don't even see a bruise."

"It's probably a bone bruise," he said. "A deep one by the feel of it. Ouch! Right there!"

She flexed and massaged his leg, and soft grateful sounds escaped his lips.

An unwanted energy drink and toilet paper tube sit on the floor. He wrings out his sweatbands and plucks little pieces of toilet paper off his face, recalling how he'd cleared his throat and knocked on Tamara's physical therapy office earlier.

"Yes?" she asked in her honeyed voice.

"I was wondering – ," Nabeet began.

Her hair fell to her shoulders and parted like stage curtains. Nabeet wanted to rehearse the song and dance between them. Nabeet, always the sweaty understudy. He adjusted his headband, feeling the perspiration already crowning his pores.

"Wondering what?"

He gulped, panicked, pointed to her crumpled energy drink can. "If you need another?"

Nabeet applies more prescription deodorant, stifling his hyperhidrosis. He makes a good Anabolix trainer, an example of how the gym can work up a great sweat. The locker room underarm and foot odors make him just another unspecial body. His forehead, a cascading dam. His palms, little rivers running off the precipices of his yellow fingertips. The waterproof nicotine patches cling to his shoulder like sinful secular badges.

The stalls on either side of Nabeet remain empty. Todd used to sit in one and keep Nabeet company while he evaporated. Todd envied Nabeet's ability to sweat – Todd had always been known for his water retention. They played in the same racquetball league. But Todd hadn't been around in a while. He'd mentioned moving. Nabeet can't blame him. Everything here must be a reminder. The league knows about Todd's suffering, his *dukkha*. Nabeet knows why he always wears the canteen, and didn't dare question it.

Nabeet has been debating an email to Todd: *We're all separated by our dukkha but also connected because of it. Buddha says nothing exists entirely alone. So if we suffer together, might we find some certainty in all that is uncertain?*

Nabeet was researching his condition at the library when he found the pamphlet "Buddhism & You" tucked into a book on the endocrine system – an obvious sign. He's learning to relinquish worldly pleasure to attain enlightenment, *bodhi*. He has concluded that his sweaty body is the result of his cigarette addiction, breaching one of Buddha's Five Basic Precepts. Nabeet makes weekly offerings at the Sangha Temple of Nirvana. But is he doing enough? He shivers. The locker room vents cool and prickle his wet skin. Maybe he should've confronted Todd about the canteen. A true Buddhist would have.

Nabeet returns to his office, releasing himself of more worldly pleasure, canceling his subscription to Kiss&Tell.com's® Virtual Cupid™ app. He remembers his last video chat, how the woman inquired about his evident and particular glisten.

But while logged in, Nabeet is Insta-Flirted™. She types how uninterested she is in his temporal descriptors: *Nervous, Damp*. She's interested in his spiritual one: *Bodhicitta*. One of Miranda315's descriptors: *Bodhisattva*. They share a goal: *Bodhicitta* being the desire for *bodhi*, and *Bodhisattva* being a person who helps sentient creatures obtain it so that all may be enlightened. *Everything is in relation to everything else,* she tells him. Her salvation depends on his. Nabeet thinks of Todd. She wants to get better acquainted before SimuDat-ing™. Miranda315 recommends the one-minute SpeakEasy™ app so they can chat without the secular distraction of flesh. Nabeet agrees, purchasing the app. He confirms, yes, he is still out there and avail-able, adjusting his computer mic, preparing to audio chat, drying his palms.

* * *

Sammy on the phone:

"Hey, kiddo."

"Dad? I'm, like, fourteen? Not a kiddo anymore?"

"Sorry, son. Just wanted to see how you're doing. How's your mother?"

"Huh? Wait. Why you asking? Do you still love her or some-thing?"

"No, no, not like that. Just being nice. She still stitching flags at the Canal Village?"

"Sure. Wait, what's wrong? You never ask about Ma like this."

"It's just a question, pal."

"Dad, I think that ship has totally sailed."

"Chet, it's just the nice adult thing to say is all. I'm nice, right?"

"Wait. What?"

"I'm not interested in your mother. Besides I'm seeing some-body."

"Hold on. Yeah?"

"Yes. Her name's Miranda. She's a divorcee, too."

"Where'd you meet Marilynn?"

"Miranda. And we haven't actually really completely officially met yet."

"Huh?"

"Well, I met her on the Internet. Through one of those sites."

"What?"

"She said I seem like a real nice guy. We don't have as much in common as she'd like. But opposites attract, I say. I think we're going to make English muffin pizzas when you and your brothers come over next time. That sound nice?"

"Dad, is this, like, a cover-up because you still love Ma? Is there really a Marilynn? Think of Ma as a ship and that ship as having, like, already totally sailed."

"You already said that, Chet."

"What? Oh, sorry. I'm playing video games with Ma's friend, Phil."

*   *   *

Felix suspects his wife is having an affair. He smelled disinfectant spray in her Honda, saw her pantyhose static-clinging to one of the headrests. Delilah slid into bed and claimed she'd exercised late due to a work conflict/function/thing. It hadn't registered, Felix half asleep, having worked the graveyard shift at MOMS: Musically Optimistic Medical Services, where he drives ambulances and makes ends meet. He and Delilah haven't been awake together in months. Now his temper prepares to tantrum, feeling cuckolded, using the computer in the MOMS drivers' lounge to register for a free account on Kiss&Tell.com® under the alias Casanova315, selecting three descriptors: *Philanderer, Casual, Unbounded.*

Felix thinks there is a system glitch when his match instantly contacts him.

Her descriptors: *Mistress, Dominatrix, Bounded.*

She Insta-Flirts™ Felix how particular she is about who ties her up. She reveals her safe word: *kazoo.* But she won't SimuDate™ until they get better acquainted, asking him to purchase the Inti-Mate™ app so they can test their role-play and fetish compatibility. Felix views her profile: the leather, the whip, the sultry snarl. Felix tugs at his collar. He figures Delilah will discover the app purchase on the credit card statement before he can exact revenge. He imagines the painful lacerations from Miranda315's whip, and says, "Kazoo." He just wanted to make Delilah cry a little and understand betrayal in a mutually cruel and self-tormenting way. Then Felix imagines Delilah crying, like at FAC High when he fell head over heels for her, and his heart breaks. He was the guy who stopped her crying, not instigated it. He logs off, telling himself he loves his wife, remembering that Delilah mentioned having to change in her car because the renovated Anabolix locker room is rumored to have peepholes.

* * *

Sammy on the phone:
"Daddy, when you were with Mommy were you in a wheelchair?"
"No, never. What kind of question is that, kiddo?"
"Chet said his Mommy said to Mommy you had trouble pulling your weight?"

* * *

Delilah applies makeup at her receptionist desk, choosing eye-liner from a drawer that contains a facedown picture of Felix. Some-times she'll eye the back of the frame and think about what he looks like, but the best she can do is recall his snoring contour in bed. She cringes at the thought of the term *divorcee*. Sammy fills her basic de-sire, her grudge. Does he think she doesn't remember how he placed that dead frog on her shoulder in biology class years ago? How she became ToadGirl for the remainder of school? Four-eyed Felix had removed the frog and let her cry into his neck while Sammy and his wideouts laughed, muting their mouths with their detention slips. But they aren't those people anymore. Felix wore contacts now per her request. Delilah puckers her lips, paints them red. She could've been more than ToadGirl. She wants to know what she should've been, what it's like to be on top.

*   *   *

Deege takes a cig break outside Kiss&Tell.com® HQ in the designated employee sidewalk smoking area while TopFlirters guffaw from their rooftop VIP butterfly veranda, flicking cig butts over the potted milkweed and marigold and lantana, pinwheeling past the office flagpole, trying to drop them into Deege's frizzy perm. When they succeed, the perm smolders. Some TopFlirters make *hawk* sounds like they're going to loogie onto Deege to extinguish the hair smoldering, but Deege knows they won't, at least not again since he tattled to Supervisor Kiel. Douchey TopFlirter Gunther had run a hand through his pompadour, explaining he wasn't aware that anybody was directly below their alleged hawking.

TopFlirters start dropping dead butterflies.

Deege returns to work.

Beyond the lobby is the Hall of Flirt – the plaques awarded quarterly to the best Kiss&Tell.com® sales proxy. Here is Supervisor Kiel engraved below Miranda607. Here is Gunther below Miranda518. Deege believes his name can be on a plaque below Miranda315 someday, thinking how the TopFlirter bonus could reinstate him at Upstate CC so he can complete his in-limbo thesis: CelebrityMugMug. com. Once successful, Deege might find a girl who'll go up on her tippy-toes to kiss him, tell him of her welling pride for his absolute greatness and just how glad she is to have found him. Deege thinks how he'd also have access to the rooftop VIP butterfly veranda, finally belonging to something.

In the elevator Deege plucks a dead monarch from his perm and recalls how he plucked spit wads from it in the orphanage stairwell. Deege was left curbside so young that he never learned to ride a bike. He only recalls the exhaust coughing as his parents drove off. Sister Lucille retrieved him from the curb. She'd smile and say, "What's not to like about you?" But as he matured, she began to say it like she was really asking.

Off the elevator Deege passes the Miranda Studios. Red lights glow above doors, indicating app sessions in progress.

Here is Katy's studio: Pictures of kids hang on the wall that don't belong to Katy, they're just the ones that came with the frames. Still, Deege tries to imagine himself up on the wall, proudly displayed like that. He peeks into the door's little window and sees Katy in a 20Q FactFinder™ session. Once, Deege asked if she'd like to 20Q FactFind™ with him over dinner. She replied, "No, thanks." She said she didn't entertain a man with no long-term goals. When Deege described CelebrityMugMug.com, she flicked her brunette bangs and coughed, but it sounded like, "*Loser.*" Deege decided he preferred blondes after that.

Here is Tila's studio: Tila engages in a SpeakEasy™ session. She tends her miniature Zen rock garden, mouthing Miranda Manual verbiage into her mic. A Buddha statue squats with meditative constipation. Incense burns.

Here is Meg's studio: Miranda's dungeon. The chained leather cuffs and whip hang, waiting for an intern to wipe with saddle soap. Behind the webcam, faded sonogram photos peel from the faux bricks. The images on them all look like the ghost of a kidney bean. This is not Miranda-related. But since it's off camera, Supervisor Kiel allows it. Once, Meg offered the staff bites of her homemade strawberry custard, and Deege was the first to raise his hand despite being allergic to dairy. He'd tried it because she'd tried it – offering with the same spoon that touched her lips – and although he'd certainly itch and swell, for one brief moment he was connected to someone. He cataloged this as a victory in his heart.

Here is Carrie's studio: Miranda's college dorm. Deege sees her twirling her blonde hair into the webcam. On screen, a man sips from something sashed to his chest. The glass fogs up, Deege wipes it. Carrie likes to comb Gunther's pompadour, finding his tan reminiscent of her Floridian youth. Deege once tried to tan, hoping to remind her of something, but only burned and peeled. He gifted her with truffles in a prototype CelebrityMugMug.com mug printed with Straw Fogel's coke-addled mug shot. But Carrie returned it, sans truffles, saying Deege was too nice to date, because she was afraid of maybe breaking his heart, but he should keep his chin up because somebody nice and special is surely out there! Deege nodded, scratching his nest of hair, recognizing her reply as verbatim Miranda Manual verbiage.

Deege enters the sales office, proxy cubicle 315. Large windows line the far wall, the mismatched carpet beneath them from last year's twister. When the staff came out of the basement, they discovered a broken window, rain-soaked carpet, and an elliptical from the gym across the street. Cars were scattered like crumpled balls of paper. Now reopened, the gym's windows show people gasping and sweating on stationary bikes. Deege practices there, trying to feel for its true balance. This, he thinks, is less humiliating than riding around his trailer park on training wheels. This, he thinks, is what life has become: a constant strategy to minimize humiliation. The flagpole juts from the bricks above the windows. Deege remembers how a doll with curly hair once hung from it all day, how Gunther and his cronies snickered from their cubicles until the janitors got around to pulling it down.

A paper airplane suddenly sticks into his hair. The fuselage windows frame crying permed passengers. Nearby cubicles chortle. Maybe shaving his head would draw less attention? He's tried gels, waxes, mousses. But the feral mop refuses to domesticate. Gunther's pompadour rises above proxy cubicle 518: that glorious slick black tsunami of frontal-lobed hair, undulating as he laughs; that barbered opus sitting up like an obedient schnauzer, begging! How does Gunther do it? Deege knows he keeps his comb in a drawer because he hears it slide open whenever Carrie stops by. He must keep his magical pomade in there, too.

Deege researches pompadour pomades, disregarding a follow-up Insta-Flirt™ from Canteen315, who apologizes for his condition in the Virtual Cupid™ session. The messages are littered with typos. Canteen315 says it was still a pleasure to meet Miranda and if she wouldn't mind telling Mindy that he'll send their son her best.

Then Canteen315 logs off.

*   *   *

Sammy climbs into Delilah's Honda. He sits in silence with his hands on his knees, the way she requires. This way, his state championship ring will glint as she drives. He has to polish it, it's mandatory. He knows nothing about Delilah except that she has a curvy flexible body that, backseated, can really contort. He isn't allowed to ask about her. She has terms. Once, she had him take her up to The Spot in the woods, where all the popular kids partied, and she fucked him on the musty couch. Sammy hadn't been up there since graduation. Just beyond the trees was a chain-link fence plastered with NO TRESPASSING posters. Beyond the fence was the precipice of the lake palisades, where a boy jumped and clipped a passing boat. Wilted flowers and disintegrated letters hung in the chain-links. Candles melted, the wax dried in long drips. Delilah slipped and called him Felix. She wore a wedding ring. She faked the orgasm. Sammy did, too. They both could tell, it all sounded different. They never went back there.

Earlier, Miranda315 told Sammy he seemed like a real nice guy and she worried that if they ignored the incompatible 20Q FactFinder™ results, she might break his heart, but he should keep his chin up because there is surely somebody special out there for him. But is he a nice guy? What kind of emotional depth did this affair require?

Sammy smells the incriminating disinfectant spray in the car. Here is his backache from a quarterback sneak against RFA, the clicking knee from a weak-side sack in the state championship game against the rival town high school, the Mighty Sputniks of Upstate. Here is the ache in his heart from the sum total of losses, of wives. He can only imagine how Delilah's husband would feel if he ever found out, because he's been there. Would a nice guy do this to somebody? What would his children think? What type of nickname would they invent then?

Delilah enters the spiral ramp of the Anabolix parking structure to an unoccupied level. Sammy is thankful for the darkness. Here is how the light on his face nearly brings him to tears.

*　*　*

After work, Nabeet knocks on Todd's door. The FOR SALE sign staked in the yard, the BEST OFFER sign in the car's windshield, the basement window near the tires littered with dings and scratches. Through the window, Nabeet spots a pair of legs. Nabeet knocks on the window. The legs shimmy. It's difficult to see through the chipped glass, so Nabeet makes a motion with his thumb toward the door. He tries the knob. It's unlocked.

"Hello?" Nabeet yells, poking his head in. His voice echoes tinny through the empty rooms. Squares of dust coat the hardwood floors where furniture used to be. Darker rectangles of paint mark the walls from pictures now unhung. Odd that there aren't any boxes. Maybe Todd has already found a new place. But why is he selling his car, too?

"Todd?" Nabeet yells, descending the staircase.

In the basement Todd stands on the dryer, reaching into the ceiling, replacing a panel.

"Hi." Todd hiccups, shivering.

"What're you doing up there?" Nabeet asks.

"Fixing a leak in a pipe," he slurs, climbing down.

The two men shake wet hands and subtly wipe them on their pants.

"Sorry to stop by like this. Been awhile. Wanted to see how you're holding up."

"You shouldn't have. But that's kind of you. Doing the best I can, I guess," Todd says.

Todd's eyes glisten, bloodshot. Ceiling pipes tick and thump.

"It's all right," Nabeet says.

"Is it?" Todd says.

"It's all right if you were crying."

Todd wipes his face. "This is sweat. You should know sweat when you see it."

Nabeet dabs his forehead with his wristband, forces a smirk.

"I'm sorry," Todd says, groaning, settling into a chair, shuffling papers at the desk. "I'm just tired." Here is Todd's computer screensaver flashing photos of TJ growing up to a certain point. Here is TJ in jazz band with his Telecaster, standing beside a boy with a huge nesty poof of hair who's holding a trombone. Miranda315 said he sounded like a really nice guy, but she didn't get the vibe that he was serious about helping all living creatures attain *bodhi.* Nabeet disagreed, though he thought of Todd and his canteen and felt caught.

"Listen," Nabeet says. "I also came by to ask a favor."

Todd shrugs. "Well, I have a lot of packing still to do."

"It's just a small favor," Nabeet says. "I need your help."

"Why me?" Todd says.

"Well, I make offerings at the Sangha Temple of Nirvana," Nabeet says, already feeling sweat on his ankles. He scratches the nicotine patches. "In order to continue toward *bodhi* I need to make more offerings." Nabeet holds up the wrinkled "Buddhism & You" pamphlet. "Fruit, food, water, or other drinks. I've already offered fruit, food, and water."

Todd hiccups.

"So I was wondering if I could offer the other drink in your canteen?"

Todd places a hand firmly over it, like pledging allegiance.

"No, no, I don't *want* it," Nabeet says. "I would never, I know it belonged –" Nabeet clears his throat. "I couldn't take it. I just need what's *inside.* To pour at the Sangha Temple of Nirvana. I don't even feel comfortable borrowing it. I could never ask."

Todd's eyes shut. Nabeet puts a hand on his shoulder. Todd startles, awakes. "Yes?"

"Maybe you could come with me? Offer for me?"

Todd sways. The scent of linens is faded like a ghost.

"Please," Nabeet says. "Help me?"

Todd blinks. "Do you know if my foundation is T-shaped or slab-on-grade?"

Nabeet looks at Todd, eyebrows up, dark with moisture.

"I should really finish fixing that lightbulb," Todd says.

"I thought you said it was a leaky pipe?"

Todd stares. Then his lower lip trembles. "All right," he sighs. "All right, let's go."

*   *   *

Gunther and the other TopFlirters head to the rooftop VIP butterfly veranda. While they are gone, Deege sneaks into proxy cubicle 518 and opens desk drawers, looking for the magical pomade. Keyboards chatter throughout the office like the teeth of cold children. Deege pokes his scalped tumbleweed. Enough is enough, he thinks.

Here is the bottom drawer of Gunther's desk, the large comb, the tube labeled "Adhairsive: Ultra-Strength Toupee Bonding Agent." Here, beneath folders, is the wooden box that holds a spare pompadour: perky and wavy and obedient.

Deege's heart clenches. He glances at the large windows.

The smell of the glue is nauseating. He recalls when he had an upset stomach and Sister Lucille sat beside him, rubbing his back as he got sick into a bedside bucket. He almost misses being that ill, those moments when somebody was there to keep him company and quell the ache that would only magnify if he had to be alone with it.

Deege smears Adhairsive over the comb's teeth, puts it back. Then he pockets the pompadour and returns to proxy cubicle 315, showing rare teeth.

Later, Gunther and the other TopFlirters return. Deege clicks Hump and Pinch and Wink LoveButtons™. He sells a few more apps and refers users to the Miranda Studios. Here is the Miranda Manual's prologue: *Nothing in Life Is Free, Why Should Love Be Any Different?* Deege thinks of the expensive truffles he gifted to Carrie and can't disagree.

Toward the end of the day, Carrie stops by proxy cubicle 518. The drawer opens. Carrie giggles as she combs Gunther's hair. Here is her strange grunt. Here is Gunther pleading, "Don't, don't, don't!" Employees appear above cubicle walls just as Carrie gives one final tug. Here is the comb in Carrie's hand, the toupee glued to it.

Carrie drops the comb and runs back to her studio, pointing into her mouth, going, *Gag!*

Gunther clutches his pale dome, his tan outlining the sideburned pompadour.

Deege waits.

But nobody laughs.

Employees just look at each other. Some stare at the floor.

Gunther's eyes well and dart around the office. He stops on Deege and lifts his eyebrows. Then he ducks down, rummaging and whimpering. Back up, he sprints to the bathroom with the wooden box tucked under an arm.

Everybody shrugs and returns to work.

Deege lets his jaw hang. Where was the laughter, the snickering, the mocking, the humiliating? How is this fair? How can he be mocked for having too much hair when Gunther has been pretending all along but actually has none?

Deege grits his teeth and marches toward the elevator.

The street begins to honk and grunt with traffic. Steam rises from the grates and reeks of garbage. He untethers the flagpole ropes. Some Kiss&Tell.com® staffers notice the flag lowering. Silhouettes appear in the windows, palms pressed against the glass. Deege uses a binder clip to attach the spare pompadour to the flag. Then he hoists.

But just before the pompadour reaches the window, Deege stops. He thinks of himself watching Gunther clutch his bald skull – how he hadn't laughed either. He recalls how Gunther's face opened and loosened as his eyes fell on Deege, unlike his usual narrowing and tightening. It was about the hair. He was jealous of Deege's hair.

Would a girl go up on her tippy-toes to kiss him for this? Is this his absolute greatness?

Sister Lucille would be ashamed.

The pompadour quivers in a breeze. Deege sees he is part of something after all.

He shudders, makes his own kind of gagging sound.

Here is how whichever rope Deege decides to pull next, which direction the pompadour moves, will relate to every moment after for the rest of his life. The Kiss&Tell.com® staffers get bored, disappear, and draw the blinds. Deege stands with the two ropes, asking himself who does he think he is? Asking like he really wants to know.

*   *   *

Delilah rides Sammy like gangbusters in the backseat of the Honda, demanding Sammy say those things she likes him to say. Sammy recites how he is going to win the big game for her, would she like to go to prom with him? Would she like to be his queen? "Oh, yes," she replies, "yes, yes, yes." She breathes onto his state championship ring like a birthday candle. Sammy feels a cramp claw up his thigh. He fits his foot comfortably between the front seats. Delilah digs in her nails, reprimands him for squirming. Sammy turns his head, thankful Delilah makes him take the little blue pill. No way is he up to this today on his own. Would a nice guy enjoy this? Delilah takes his hand and stamps it over a breast.

"Squeeze gentle but firm, like you're going to throw a screen pass," she orders.

"We need to stop," Sammy says.

"You know how this goes," she scolds.

Sammy tries to sit up but Delilah pins him down. The cramp shoots up his side – a full-throttled charley horse. Sammy bucks in pain. Delilah hoots. Sammy kicks the leg out and bumps the gearbox into neutral. Delilah and Sammy tumble to the floor shrieking as the Honda rolls backward down the spiral ramp of the parking structure.

*   *   *

Carpooling to the Sangha Temple of Nirvana, Canteen feels the liquid sashed to his chest slosh whenever the car jostles. He sips between potholes. Nabeet reminds him to save some for the offering. He gives Nabeet a crooked thumbs-up, joints hurting too much to turn fully upright. He'd make this gesture after announcing a chord that TJ strummed clean. He recalls little TJ with his scout neckerchief falling across the apex of his back like a small cape. Canteen fingers one of the fraying scout badges, keeping his wet, burning eyes forward. He thinks of the antsy noose in his ceiling, like the skeleton of a teardrop.

*   *   *

Nabeet recalls Miranda315 telling him it's important not to see yourself separate from others. But hadn't Miranda315 separated herself from him? Isn't that very *unBodhisattvalike*? What if it's just a hoax? What if it's impossible to alleviate *dukkha*? Nabeet's armpits begin to tingle with moisture. What if he's just a lonely, sweaty guy?

Several potholes jostle Nabeet and Todd. The men let themselves be moved.

Nabeet idles at a red light, sucking his fingertips, remembering his secret stash.

Maybe just one more cigarette? he thinks. Can't make things worse.

He reaches for the glove box when Todd gasps. Nabeet looks up. A runaway blue Honda rolls backward out of the gym's parking structure. It crosses the street and collides with a mailbox. Letters burst into the air like feathers from an exploded goose, and several envelopes fall onto Nabeet's windshield. He flips on the wipers. The sound of the crash instantly geysers his pores. Then he sees it. Todd is already standing outside of the car. The crash's reverberation has jostled a large potted plant off a rooftop that's falling toward a boy's poof of hair.

*   *   *

Here is the thud, the crack, the burst of white. Deege notices he's on his back looking up at the potted milkweed and marigold of the rooftop VIP butterfly veranda. But the lantana is missing. Winged things flutter and bob. Something pale and smooth and round reflects sunlight in the space where a potted plant should be. Then it's gone.

Deege tries to get up but can't. Something is off. A memory: Deege sitting on a bike, pedaling. A palm rests on his back, guiding him forward. Over Deege's shoulder, a man with identical hair jogs at his side, steadying the seat with his other hand. A soft push and suddenly he's on his own, feeling the give-and-take of his centered weight, of gravity. But when Deege looks back to see if the man is watching, the handlebars wobble, and before he can correct, he's falling. A shoelace wraps around the bike's gear, pinning him beneath the frame. Deege cries out, staring straight up. The burn of a scraped knee. He waits and cries and waits and cries, but the man who looks just like him never comes.

Instead, a barrel-torsoed man appears with a canteen sashed up where his heart should be, and an athletic glistening Indian in a soggy shirt. Deege asks for the man who looks just like him, but his dry mouth only makes a guttural noise. Something is definitely off. His heart pounds. The sun is bright. The pavement feels warm but his toes are cold. The canteened man teeters and groans, getting down onto his knees. The Indian's sneakers go *squish squish squish*. Maybe a hydrant exploded. The Indian dials a phone with his yellow fingertips. The phone pops out of his grasp like a slick fish. Maybe he's calling a tow truck for the blue car. Maybe it's not even a phone. Deege can't move his neck. He can only use his peripherals.

"It's fine," the canteened man slurs. His hot breath burns Deege's nostrils.

Deege notices that it feels like he's clutching something furry.

Why am I still on the ground? Deege wonders. Something is off.

"It's fine, you'll be fine this time," the man says.

A hint of lantana in the breeze. More voices mumble. A crowd forms. Somebody says, "Is that – ?" Another says, "Wow, I think so. I mean, look at his hair!" Deege blushes, wondering if Gunther and the TopFlirters put something in his perm again. He tries to move and feels sick, his head erupting. His eyes fill with pinkish tears.

"Oh, God," the canteened man hiccups. He looks up, "Somebody call Mindy!"

"Don't leave me," Deege is able to muster. He's not sure if he's going to be sick.

The man turns back. "You'll be fine, TJ. I'm here."

Didn't he go to school with a TJ? Weren't they in jazz band together? Deege was a novice and took up an instrument to avoid any additional time absorbing spit wads. Luckily, his mop of hair prevented him from fitting into lockers. But even band members snarled, saying Deege worked his trombone slide as if he were masturbating the instrument. Except TJ. Whenever Deege hit a correct note, TJ lifted a crooked thumbs-up that was so certain in itself. Deege defined possibility by that crooked thumb.

Deege trembles. "Please, just stay."

"I'm here," the canteened man says. "I'm not going anywhere." The scent of rubbing alcohol. Is the man cut? His hand is all bloody. Deege opens his mouth and pain shoots down his neck. This time his mouth feels wet and sour.

"Please, stay with me. I don't feel so good. Something's off," Deege sobs.

"You're doing fine. Help's coming."

The Indian is asking for water. A nearby car idles.

Here is how Deege hears the muffler cough: *Loser Loser Loser.*

A man and woman appear from the backseat of the blue car, where Deege swears a mailbox is supposed to be. The man and woman form the far side of the crowd. "Is he – ?" the woman says, touching her mussed hair. The man's shirt is on inside-out and unbuttoned, his hairy belly sagging. The man places his hand on the woman's shoulder. She turns and presses up against him, going up on her tippy-toes to cry into the crook of his neck. And the man holds her, keeps her close. How nice, Deege thinks. How nice.

Deege shuts his eyes. Just for a moment, he decides.

Droplets sting his forehead. He opens his eyes. The canteen up close. The desert camouflage pattern. The duct tape is peeling, and behind it a hole. The expanding wet spot on the man's shirt indicates a second hole, an exit wound.

The man picks a hunk of terra-cotta from Deege's frizzy mop.

A ringing in Deege's ears. Or maybe it's the jingle of a MOMS ambulance siren.

Then the pain swells up, like cymbals behind his eyes.

"Please, don't leave me!"

"Listen to me," the canteened man says. "You'll be fine. I'm right here with you. I'm not going to leave your side this time, I promise."

Here is how Deege believes him.

Here is a forgotten balance revisited.

Tornadic

After work I'd have a new message from Meg, telling me where she found them that morning. Backs of her knees, her armpits, the buttocks. Like dawn horizons breaking all over her. I wondered if the paper cuts were really paper cuts or that thing a woman does when she talks about paper cuts but is really talking about something else. I could take a good guess at what the something else was. Except she didn't talk about that. She sounded different on the phone. Like what a canyon would boomerang in echo.

Either way, I called back. But the line just beeped that disconnected number beep.

Probably wouldn't have recognized me if she'd kept her old number and answered. My voice had baritoned in the year since we spoke. I had packed on a few. Blame the hair of the dogs. I'd drink so much red wine it looked like I had blood in my teeth. Took it to the bowling alley in diet soda cans. Least I quit smoking. Cigs masked the stink of the pipes I cleaned out. After she left I started hawking appliances for Fundamentals. Better pay than plumbing. Everything had that new smell. But I had to wear a tie. All I did for nine hours was stand and itch beneath my collar, imagining getting my paws around that snipe called Success. Then I punched out, got beers and a lane at the Bowl-O-Drome, finding some respite from it all, collapsing what the pinsetter deposited in a perfect white grin in front of me.

I'd stumble home, dizzy and untied, and get messages like this:
There's a single one on my left earlobe.

Dale, I've got tally marks on my inner thighs this morning. Eight total.

I found a tiny hand on my belly. A square palm and cuts for little fingers.

She cried after *fingers*. I touched my belly when it growled from hunger and figured it to be something close to the same. I bit my lip to fend off the tears.

I must've replayed that particular message at least a dozen times.

Meg and I met on a routine job. I could tell she was divorced by the clog in her drain. Rinds of rotten martini fruit, jewelry, short blond hairs. She had long flocks of red. Her crooked front teeth complemented the gaps in mine, and I thought of the word *collateral*. She could make me rub my legs together like a raptured cricket. She sighed and gripped my hair in a way that made me believe I was capable of releasing the agonies and ghosts blocking her heart. 'Course I wore rubbers. My father took off before I was born. I didn't want to go through the rigmarole of believing I could be a father. Like I knew a thing or two.

Burned the candle just shy of six months. But six months isn't six months sometimes. I know the secret to her family's strawberry custard. Used to push down on her lower back, like I was giving her CPR, to crack her spine. There was always a pressure in her that needed releasing. Her hobby was peeling dead skin off my feet. Never broke wind in front of each other, though. I peed with the door closed and the faucet running.

Days after she dumped me, I went to her complex and knocked till my fists hamburgered. Her car was in the lot. I wouldn't have taken me back either. She changed her locks, refused to come out. When neighboring tenants started poking their heads into the hallway, I got the heck out of there.

I waited by the phone for a week. Then I took up drinking because I didn't like the taste of it. I felt the need to acquire some dignity, humility. I quit cigs because the smell reminded me of her headaches. I took up bowling to replace the weight of her.

Who knows where she is now, vacant and manifesting. Borrowed a caller ID machine from Steve in Electronics, but the number she'd been calling from flashed RESTRICTED. I couldn't *69. She wasn't in the phone book.

At the Bowl-O-Drome townies nicknamed me General Howitzer for how hard I slung the ball. I lacked finesse. Just threw with sheer force, willing my torment onto the pins. Almost bowled a perfect game that way once. The lane awarded me a placard under the 275 CLUB between the popcorn machine and arcade games. It was shameful, my name on display like that. People seeing it and thinking I must feel some sense of accomplishment. Like it was anything to be proud of. I pulled it off the wall and pitched it into the dumpster.

*　*　*

When I returned the caller ID to Steve in Electronics, he asked me again to rethink his bowling team. He noticed my Bowl-O-Drome placard before I could toss it. Steve's polka-dotted tie was always short. My pop sold insurance, said a salesman built a career around the knot of his tie. I wore clip-ons till I learned a crisp Windsor. Steve's daughter's cat had birthed a litter, and his big appeal for flat-screens was a two-year warranty plus a free kitten. I told him no again. I didn't bowl because I liked it. It had to do with watching that white grinning triangle break. Leave me to my release and my Generaling and my Howitzering and what little admiration or jealousy I can muster from complete strangers watching me go.

"What if I threw in a free kitten?" Steve asked. "Would that sweeten the pot?"

He tugged on his short tie. It was so pathetic I almost said, Yes, yes it would.

But I told him no thanks and returned to Appliances.

Fundamentals liked my plumbing background. Refrigerators are all pipes and valves and heat exchanges. It's about temperature and pressure. But I was a bottom-feeder like Steve. I hadn't made a sale in a month. There was no competition in me.

In Appliances someone had leaned against one of the Subzero models with slick stainless steel panels. I found a handprint. I imagined Meg weeping, waking up to find the paper cut fingers on her belly. I grabbed a rag and polished till it was gone.

*   *   *

Last time I saw her, she was sobbing in her empty bathtub.

Meg clutched these two blankets: one pink with flowers, the other blue with a rocket ship. I figured they were from the shoe box in her closet filled with little clothes for the dolls she had lined up on the shelf above her bed. I sat on the tub ledge and touched her knee. It was prickly. She didn't get shy about it like normal. It wasn't until after I started bowling that it made sense. I grew this neck beard. But I looked in the mirror and never saw it.

She flicked a piece of lint off the rocket ship and said she'd carried it for eight months. Today it would have been three. She told the doctors not to tell her the particulars about boy or girl. Somehow knowing would have made it worse.

"The cake would've said Alice. Or Asher," she said to me.

Whenever I bowled, striking, guttering, hardly sparing, my ball would return to me out of this dark pipe, slick and cold, and I'd sweat right through my shirt till my bones showed, thinking of her carrying that man's child. What she told me and showed me in the pictures she hadn't torn or burned. The baseball cap shading all of his face except the natural frown. His hands in his pockets, shoulders hunched as if bothered. If she didn't open her legs she couldn't be worth a damn, he'd said. They'd all fuck her but never love her. Etc.

I'd scratch where the beard sprouted across my throat. I felt scooped out. The half-eaten carton of homemade strawberry custard still freezer-burning in my high-performance Maytag. Everything is pipes. Ones that work and ones that don't.

The faucet leaked in the tub. I meant to replace the aerator and valve seat and washers, but it slipped my mind. A small puddle formed near the drain. She touched her toe to a drop clinging to the faucet and pulled it away with her.

It was killing me to look at. I couldn't take it.

"Lots of women have them," I said, "miscarriages."

She pressed the baby blankets to her face. I'd showered but couldn't smell the cigarettes on me anymore. I was always worried I reeked of other people's pipes. I didn't want to give her another headache. So I left her there and waited on the couch.

Later, she locked the bathroom door and said she wanted to sleep alone tonight.

By the time I got home, she'd left me a message.

What we had was not what I thought, she said. *I just can't do this.*

*   *   *

"Like Fourth of July!" Roger said from the bar. He was a roofer with thick, tarry fingers and sunburned ears. His pal Selick nodded. Selick had taken shrapnel in Iraq. Wore this special bowling attachment on his wrist – a three-pronged instrument with corks. Now he had the cup-holder prosthetic strapped on and was blowing the foam off his beer. I'd sit with them after their league, drinking, never really liking them. All they did was complain about their women. It was all toilet seat ups and downs and throw pillow woes with those two.

"The General's at it again!" Bruce proclaimed. He was retired. His mouth was too small for his head. I don't want to look that lonesome at sixty. Had a five-year plan I kept putting off. There was this lakeside property I had my eye on. Nice view of the palisades, where that boy fell off. Enough yard for a mutt to run, a kid or three. If the wife wanted a couple chickens, I could build a coop. It was just agony to imagine sometimes.

"Watch! He'll sic the howitzer on that kindling down there between the moats! Watch him punch out Grandma's dentures!"

I waited for the ball to return. I opened my palms to the gusts of the automatic dryer. The carpeting smelled musty and had asterisk burns from cigarettes. Most townies used their own balls, polished till they could pick their teeth clean in the reflections. Me, I just used the dulls available from the racks. Then I Fourth-of-Julyed the place. It was the eighth frame. I let fly and the pins ricocheted and scattered like a firework.

In the ninth frame they said it was like I was gifting hurt on the helpless.

In the tenth, like I was fashioning thunder.

"You've merged pressure systems, young How!" Roger said as I left.

Outside, real summer storms shook their vendettas. I walked under soldered clouds and zippers of light, lowering my head into the wind. People used faucets, opened fridges, never gave me a thought. What type of life is that? I carried home the thunder of pins and clouds and impotencies, wrung out my socks as Meg's next message played:

Dale, I took Ambien to really knock myself out. But I still woke up with tic-tac-toe on the bottoms of my feet. Xs won. I'm walking like a penguin. Remember how you were always the X? Remember when we played on the train from Philadelphia?

Philly has this humidity where your fingers bloat so you keep making fists. Had a copy of our local *Upstate Sentinel*. We filled the margins with tic-tac-toe, clacking out of 30th Street Station. She claimed she kept losing because she let me have the center square out of affection. The rain let up. The car smelled of vinyl and decline.

She pointed to a headline: BOY FALLS FROM PALISADES, DISAPPEARS.

"Poor kid," I responded, plotting my next *X*.

"Poor kid," Meg said. She looked out the window and touched where a raindrop trembled on the other side of the pane. She mentioned the boy's parents, but I had already moved on to the daily Jumble, unscrambling *hyphenate,* then *lawnmower.*

I'd spin my childhood pet turtle on its shell and call it break dancing. Once, I forgot to flip it back over and found it petrified. That was my closest stint as a parent. I buried it in a coffee can in Mom's landscaping. Still, I had no clue about grief like hers.

I stopped the answering machine. Wine in the cupboard. I contemplated another blackout, thought about bowling again, but I was out of diet soda cans. Rainwater dripped through my fingers. Sometimes when the hangovers passed and I stopped coughing into the sink, I rubbed my hand along my hairy gut and stuck a finger in the bellybutton, trying to imagine kicks and a heartbeat. It's just pitiful, these things: empathy and creation.

Without that ex of hers, where might we be? I used to call her my MegPie.

She had never been one to lie. Pinky swears were legally binding contracts. One time I pinky-swore her I'd check on the casserole while she was in the shower, and when the oven started to smoke, she didn't speak to me for the rest of the day. But still, how could anyone have that many paper cuts? So I took a receipt from my pocket and ran it over my fingertip until I felt a thin sting. A drop of blood bloomed and a warmth carried, knuckle by knuckle, burning through my wrist and elbow, working its way in in in.

Then I gave myself another on the pinky.

I rinsed my hand under the sink. That's when I thought about her drain, what I discovered in there at the beginning of us. Imagine all the things I left behind there: the unfiltered cigarette butts, the black stubble, the matches. Imagine some plumber taking a look at those pipes, what he might pull out, what he might compile and think of me.

*   *   *

I couldn't sleep. I took a sick day and kept going back and forth between the couch and the bed until the phone rang.

"You picked up," Meg said.

She worked at an Internet dating company. Went by "Miranda" there. She always came home smelling of saddle soap. I wanted to ask if she could still smell it on herself, but I didn't. She was just another stranger now.

I traced the mouth of the phone with my finger. "So," I said.

"So," she said. "So, so, so."

"How's work?"

"Work is work is work is work," she said.

I thought about making a joke to lighten the mood, or asking about her mother.

Her phone-static breaths were driving me up the wall and into the light fixture.

"I hear you quit plumbing?" she said.

She was still close by enough to get wind of the grapevine, or the grave gripes. One of her friends was dating one of mine from the union who now did home installations for Fundamentals. I didn't ask about her. Couldn't bring myself to find out if some new man had his dead-skinned feet up on her coffee table.

"*Quit* makes it sound like a bad thing," I said, already accusing her.

She didn't answer.

"Well," I began but hadn't thought beyond that.

"You seeing anybody?"

"Maybe," I said. "Maybe not."

I moved my finger as if to play with the phone cord. But it was wireless.

She exhaled and static exploded. "I can't talk long," she said.

"Got plans?" I asked, sick in the gut.

"Maybe," she snapped. "Maybe not."

"Fine," I said. "Why don't you just tell me where you found them this time?"

"Underneath my breasts," she said.

I thought of the mole above her hip, its feel and shape. The Alamo, I called it.

"Want me to come over there and burn all your paper for you?"

She snorted. "Mr. Fix-it."

I got hot in the face. That tone of hers.

"I'm the one who pounded on your door," I said. "Fists swelled up so bad you couldn't even see the knuckles. So don't do me any favors."

I didn't know what that last part meant. I was breathing heavy. I sort of hoped she'd hung up. I hated myself for that cowardice.

Then my gut dropped.

She laughed. One I'd never heard from her. I felt like a pet. The phone grew heavier. Didn't know she was capable of such a thing. Didn't know what I was capable of. Didn't know much of anything about anything, really.

"I didn't answer the door because I had paper cuts all over my *face*. And fingers. I didn't want you to see me like that. I didn't think you'd give up so quick. I couldn't dial the phone or type. I called in sick. My therapist thought I should let you know."

"Why is your therapist talking about me?"

The way she was swallowing. I still knew what that meant. I loosened.

"That child grew inside me. You have no idea what I've been through."

She was right. I wanted to help. Her in that tub. But I'd named what had happened to her with blunt force. Said the word as if I'd earned the right or could know it as my own. Like it could've been any word. *Garage, coupon, hyphenate, lawnmower.*

My fingers went numb. I couldn't remember the last time I shivered like that. Not since the '92 snowstorm, its cutting wind chills and drifts. Headlights wandering, engines stalling. Her body couldn't hold it in. And all I was doing was touching my gut in the mirror and listening to my blood tick. Like I could know her loss or wanting.

What could I say?

"Trick to your strawberry custard is tart rhubarb. Don't think I didn't care."

But she'd already cut the line. That disconnected conversation beep.

* * *

I took the bus to the alley and snagged two lanes and two pitchers. Most shots rattled into the gutters. I didn't keep score. Just threw as hard as I could till my tendons could've snapped and coiled up into my biceps like frightened rabbits.

Sure don't baby the ball. Could almost hear Bruce. *Don't think the General's capable of sympathy! Don't think he's capable of a careful release!*

Congratulations on Your Martyrdom!

This time each day I was at Fundamentals, leaning against the refrigerators eating a KwikStop sandwich, playing with the price tags and fantasizing a murderous victory over something, or watching sports highlights on the fifty different-size TVs in Steve's department. A daytime league competed beside me. These townies didn't know my infamy and watched curiously as I fired and sweated. Mechanics versus janitors. The Upstate Motors name patches read WROBEL and KOWALCZYK and MAJEWSKI.

I could almost hear Bruce: *Gifting hurt on the helpless is what it is.*

Her, giving me second thoughts, thought after thought after thought.

Her openings, opening, opening.

Hard as I could, I let go. The ball kicked out of the gutter and bounced across several lanes, sounding like a gavel in a courtroom. The ball hit the league pins. The janitors and mechanics stopped. They looked at me, the pins, then each other. A small argument escalated. Finally, a pudgy janitor came over. His name patch was stitched with IAN.

"I *had* a good game going there, chump," he said. "Turns out I got to play that. There's no reset in league play. You might've cost us our season. We were down a blown rail spare already. Plus we got stuck with bed posts in another frame."

The bags under his eyes looked like bruises. I wanted to feel sorry.

But I just couldn't give a good goddamn.

"Pity about the 7–10," I sighed. "More a pity you jagged a basic spare like a turd."

His face squared, fists curling into perfect callused machines. More knuckles than Jesus. Yes! I thought. Please! Make it count!

Just one little snicker and he was on me slugging the air out. My lungs felt like plastic grocery bags. I thought of Meg. I leaned in, turned so he had fresh places to punish. The blood in my head squealed, my teeth felt loose in my skull, and everything got muffled the way it does when you yawn real hard.

Ian's teammates took their time coming over. Fine by me. The high school kid at the shoe rental counter just held the nozzle on a can of disinfectant, bug-eyed. Indoor clouds formed. The bartender on call made it to me at the same time as the other janitors. He lifted me up and dusted my shoulders. I wheezed. My neck hurt if I raised an arm above my head. I squinted. The bartender pressed his dishrag to my pulsing face. The janitors chugged their beers and laughed, slapping Ian on his back as they walked out.

"You square?" the bartender asked. "How many fingers I got up?"

He held up two fingers. I held up two fingers.

*   *   *

Toward the end of the next day, I spotted Steve shuffling over to me in a hurry, and I thought if he tried to entice me onto the bowling team again with a kitten, I'd feed it to him. But he didn't. Didn't even acknowledge the Band-Aids, the fat eyebrow that bulged like a duck egg ready to hatch, the swollen lower lip that kept feeling pinched. Steve was pale and sweaty, and his eyeballs were about ready to pop out of his head.

"You see what's going on?" he gasped.

I shrugged. He took me by the bruised wrist. I winced. He didn't notice.

In Electronics some of the fifty televisions were broadcasting the local meteorologist, Kurt Metropolis, as he assembled a squall line of lightning bolts and dark clouds and spirals over a magnetic map of our county. The other televisions played sports highlights and commercials and daytime soaps. But all the televisions had the yellow ISOLATED SUPERCELL WATCH banner streaming across the bottoms of the screens.

Closed-captioning couldn't keep up with Kurt's jabbering. His mouth moved and jutted and tensed. *Warm front, cold front, collision, clockwise, counterclockwise, occluded front* made it onto the screen. It was then that I noticed the rain on the roof. Sounded like when a boiler explodes and all the water rushes out of the pipes.

The banners turned TORNADO WARNING red.

The camera cut to Tuxedo trailer park at the outskirts of town. A reporter leaned into the gusts, shielding her face, poncho battered with hail. Little chunks bounced off her head. Stalks of corn were snapping off. Anvil-shaped clouds hunkered and breathed, little fingers poking down from their undersides. Branches of lightning burned the sky.

My head ached, concussed or hungover or both.

"Those aren't – ?" I said.

Goose bumps rose and stung my neck and arms. Customers and workers gathered around. Mike from Washers/Dryers, Tanya from Bed & Bath, Jeff from the Garden Center. Probably more, but I turned back just in time to see a fat thumb poke down from a cloud, this chimney of dark smoke lowering, lower, lower, till it hit the cornfield.

Then it got blacker, wider. The rain stopped.

All of the televisions switched over to their station's meteorologist.

The banners: F4 SPOTTED. SEEK IMMEDIATE SHELTER.

A siren rioted through the mall that I'd never heard.

The PA clicked on. "*Code Black, Code Black, Code Black!*" someone announced.

People scrambled and panted and panicked. One woman grabbed handfuls of soda bottles. A few dropped and foamed. Somebody else climbed into a tent in Outdoors. Eli from the Portrait Studio actually punched out before running around the revolving door three times. I just loosened my tie and watched the big funnel move.

Steve trembled. "My daughter's at school!" He tried to call, but the line just beeped that busy signal beep.

The wall of televisions loomed over us, strobing the same flash of lightning at separate times because of the stations' varying feed delays. Weather teams showed the black twister move out of the trailer park. One television filmed a lamppost wrench perpendicular. Another caught a trailer implode and flip. The siding tangled and spun like a child's pinwheel. Up in the corner, orchard trees uprooted. A reporter clung to the underside of a park bench. The television directly in front of me showed a fire truck tip over, its ladder tearing down some power lines. On the television beside it, all the lights went out in the houses behind a reporter holding on to the hood of his raincoat. A huge high-def flat-screen on the top row filmed the tornado sidle up to the Bowl-O-Drome and rubble the façade. And I thought of her armpits, her nape, beneath her breasts, just boards and asbestos and dead neon and me.

Steve sat on the floor with his hands on his head. The thing had hips and strutted. It tantrumed like a toddler. It headed in the direction of the school and Upstate Gardens Apartments. I had smoked on that fire escape, watching the sunset over the west acre of orchard. I could hear Meg humming through the window, smelling the garlic. I burned everything I cooked. Once, I walked in and found her staring at her mail, the thick phone book and Fundamentals catalog stacked on a chair. She had tears in her eyes.

It shifted again.

Different news crews kept tabs. Cars skidded off the road, trash cans rolled around, branches and satellite dishes and swing sets cartwheeled about. It went right through a small neighborhood and turned everything into cornflakes.

All fifty televisions showed the mall from different angles, the parking lot, Anabolix gym and the business complex across the street. Cars lifted into the storm and were spat out as crumpled diet soda cans. A red pickup with an Upstate Motors decal on the door rattled on its axles before all of the TVs went to static. The lights flickered.

Then the red pickup came crashing through the front of the store.

Revolving door glass exploded, wind roared inside my ears, my hair pushed so hard it stung at the roots, dirt and gravel scratched my cheeks, the lights cut and the floor rumbled, a sweat broke behind my ears, my arms burned, a pulse throbbed in my eyeballs, the swollen one ready to burst. Still, I envied the ability of the thing.

I grabbed Steve and we booked it to Appliances.

People were climbing into washers, dryers, freezers. Me and Steve yanked out the shelving of an industrial fridge and shut ourselves inside. Wind howled and whistled, flecks of debris knocked against the paneling, then several heavy bangs. Steve sobbed. What if his daughter was at recess, on the swings or hopscotching, and she got speared by a flying fence post? His tie was the right length today, his knot a crisp, fat triangle. His breath reeked of muddy break room coffee. It terrified me. I still might have a chance, too.

"I need to get to my little girl!" Steve cried.

He opened the fridge and tried to scramble out. I got him around the waist. Blenders and speakers and shoes slid along the aisles. The refrigerator walls flexed. Pressure squeezed my eardrums. Wind roared like the trains that flattened and stretched pennies I put on the rails as a boy. I liked to stand close to the tracks and feel it in my ears. Had a jar of yawning Lincolns hidden under my bed because Mom said pennies caused derailments. Mama, I'm not ready to die! I hugged Steve closer. I couldn't let go. His daughter should have more years than me. I thought of children younger than her at the school, more years yet. Then I thought of babies.

That's when I cried.

My ears popped, coming so close.

Steve looked up. The roof tore off. The sky swirled black hot electric.

I saw the inside of it.

ELBOW

HUMERUS

Ian's mother warned him about jumping on the mattress.

"You'll hurt your head," she sighed. "I've had enough hurt heads in my life."

She was too tired to scold him. His father had been the stern one, a housepainter with spattered jeans and fingers stinking of turpentine. If Ian disobeyed, he did the spanking. Then the doctors found a white splotch on his brain. So now Ian tucked his hands beneath his armpits and flapped and clucked and jumped on the bed.

His mother took him to the petting farm the week after the funeral. "For fresh air," she said. It was warm out but she hugged herself. Chickens flapped, hovering just above the ground. Ian asked why chickens couldn't fly. What was wrong with them?

"Nothing," she said. "They're just too heavy. They're carrying too much weight."

Trails of old tears overlapped his mother's cheeks for days at a time. She never wiped them off. Why bother? It was like making his bed, Ian thought. Why would he make his bed if he was just going to sleep in it again later?

He jumped higher, harder. He tried to slap the ceiling, high-five his father. Maybe he'd come back and spank Ian so hard the handprint would smell like turpentine. He wanted to see if his mother would get mad. Or would she stay in her room with the curtains

97

drawn, looking through photo albums, spraying his father's cologne on the couch, on pillows, on shirts she'd crumple and toss on the floor beside the laundry basket?

Ian mistimed a jump. He landed on the floor with his hands still tucked beneath his armpits and broke his elbows. The doctor found a damaged ligament near the humerus, though Ian didn't feel like laughing. It felt like someone was holding matches under his funny bones. Thick white casts wrapped his arms. They looked like wings. His friends played tic-tac-toe on them. Someone wrote *Pocket Pool Injury* and Ian wasn't sure what it meant, or why the other kids found it so funny, or why his teacher had to scribble it out.

During Career Day, boys were casts of their fathers. Men talked about a good work ethic. The school janitor discussed solvents for gum wads and paint. He partnered with Ian while fathers made macaroni crafts with their sons and daughters.

ULNA

Sometimes Marie sang to him under the sheets. "I have thin vocal cords," she said. "I'm a natural falsetto." She sang in a choir. Ian could pick her voice out of the tenors and sopranos and baritones. She whispered songs into his ear and bit his neck. They inspected their bodies after sex, as if they might have transformed during, touching palms and comparing finger lengths, placing forearms side by side. The length of the forearm is equal to one cubit, she'd learned years ago in church school. "Your cubit is bigger than my cubit," Marie said. She worked at the Laundromat and said you could really learn about someone by their stains. You could know them, what they liked, what they lacked, what they were going through. Food stains were a sign of some sort of loss. Ink equaled workaholic. "Coffee stains more times than not mean a smoker trying to quit," she said. "You could tell if they succeeded or not by the yellow nicotine smudges or burns." One time, while comparing cubits, she stopped and pointed to a pale scar above one of his elbows. "How'd you get this?" she asked.

"Childhood accident."

She kissed the scar. "What'd you do?"

"Something my father told me not to," he said and looked out the window.

She left it at that. Early on, she'd seen the old picture in his wallet: Ian as a child with a man painting a wall. The man had bright yellow paint on his roller. Ian pushed his clean roller along the carpet like a lawnmower. "Is this your father?" she asked.

Ian nodded.

"I bet you're a lot like him," she said.

Ian shrugged and tucked the wallet under the mattress.

Months later they were walking down the sidewalk when Ian bumped into a man carrying a package marked FRAGILE. The box fell, something shattered. The man cursed and shoved Ian. Ian clenched his hands. He'd never been in a fight. He wasn't aware of the proper fist technique, and tucked his thumbs under his fingers. The man noticed, calmed. "You'll break your thumbs swinging that way, dummy," he said, and walked away laughing. Ian blushed. Marie looked down the street and watched traffic start and stop.

She moved out west to try her luck at singing. She said she couldn't get those fists out of her head. Ian puked after finding one of her hair clips in the medicine cabinet. He was a janitor at the mall and called in sick for a week, skipped bowling league. The medicine cabinet mirror made it all worse. Pieces of his mother stared back. So did pieces of someone else, pieces that became less specific every day, less genetic, more generic. He gained weight, felt a pulling down. His fists grew rounder and softer. He ate in bed, staining the sheets. He took them to the cleaners and wondered if they might be able to tell what had happened and, terrified, he never picked them up. Instead, he bought brand-new linens.

RADIUS

It was sometime after the storm. Things were being weathered.

Marie came back, her middle ballooned. She put on weight, too, he thought.

"I'm pregnant," she said. "I can't be a singer looking like this."

Ian rubbed the back of his neck. "Is it mine?"

She blinked, looked down. "I don't know. Maybe. I've been gone a while."

Ian put a hand to his lips and pushed his mouth around.

Marie wept. "I'm scared. I don't know what to do. I can't do this alone."

He watched her, now one and a half of herself. She showed him the sonogram, and he saw a little white smudge and maybe the same big forehead he saw in his mirror each morning, the forehead his mother did not have. He looked at the smudge closer.

"It's a girl," Marie said.

He looked up, then reached out and touched her stomach.

The child kicked. Ian recoiled, his eyebrows lifted.

She placed her hand on his stomach. "Ian, you've let yourself go."

So he started running. When Marie stopped by, Ian rubbed lotion on her belly. She had new songs to sing him, lullabies. He thinned, his features regained their shape. A jawline, a waistline, old hairline-fracture scars. By the time the baby arrived, he had nearly lost all of the excess weight. Marie dropped the child off and Ian held her in the crook of an arm. She fit perfectly there. Her little backbone, the length of his forearm. One cubit tall, he thought. Such a tiny person! Fuzzy head! Whenever she made fists, Ian untucked the thumb and placed it outside the other fingers. The child squealed and cooed. She weighed almost nothing. She would never weigh this little again, he thought. The earth would just keep pulling.

But he could help bear some of it, he realized, cradling her. His funny bone tingled. The damaged ligament had been repaired. It could turn and bend like everyone else's, but his arm could never fully straighten. Now, with the shared weight of the child, it was enough to stretch that ligament and open his joint, extend it.

Later his doctor gave a thumbs-up to his waist, his loss, checking the strength of his heart through a stethoscope. "You had me worried there for a while," he said. Ian stood in his underwear. His elbows jutted away from his body. The doctor said this was a deviation, described it as a pronounced *carrying angle*. Some people were born with it, sometimes it occurred after a childhood incident, an injury during development.

"But what does it mean?" Ian asked.

The doctor shrugged. "If anything," he said, "it means you can carry more."

KARST

The wall alarm buzzes, which means another shipment of fatty epidermises has arrived, which means I get on the phone to Porcine, Bovine, and Marine and advise: Prep to intake. Then I'll call down to Labs and advise: Initiate collagen and tallow extraction.

Below my office, the docked semitrucks unload parcels of skin. I gag, distract myself with the svelte of my plastic terrarium, and coochie-coochie-coo a leaf. The Complexion department thinks I took the divorce bad, that I've got unTylenoled diaper fever. As a joke, Larson got me a baby thermometer. I use it as a coffee stirrer. But the terrarium had been a gift from Doreen in Archives. "Look," she said after my divorce hit the grapevine. "I glued a rubber lizard to the tank. Thought you could use a little color. The north end of the building doesn't get direct sunlight." Often, Doreen touched her forehead wrinkles in her computer screen reflection. This confirmed my fondness. I worry about my own crow's feet and eye tic. Tara and I didn't share something self-conscious like that. She was flawless down to the piggy toe. She moved away with a rigid Italian dentist who ends all his words in vowels.

My favorite part of the day is filing the Transport Discharge. I check the semis' license plates: Oklahoma, Utah, Montana. Since last year, I've been to Mount Rushmore and Niagara Falls. I like that I can go back and they'll be waiting for me. On a gas station map I draw lines over the highways I've driven. I stir my coffee with the baby thermometer, sweating whenever I imagine Tara making the

Italian moan *That-a Feels-a so Good-o!* My eye twitches, recalling how my neighbor wept over his wife's coffin, his children's, cursing the maybe-deer that darted in front of their car. I'm nauseous by the lot possibility.

I used to send Doreen notes with the Transport Discharges, like, *On the sea of life you're my soul matey!* She saved the Post-its in her desk. Then Clint from Rejuvenation started showing up, stretching her forehead skin and saying, "See, see?" And she lifted her eyebrows, saying, "Yes, I do see!" I reported Clint's behavior to Dengle, but he said, "Randolph, what is it we manufacture here?" To which I replied, "Cosmetics?" To which he corrected, "Try *beauty*? We're already the bridesmaid to Maybelline. What kind of president would I be if I stuck my schnoz into personal affairs and disrupted something beautiful?"

So I phoned Clint and called dibs, advising: Back off.

To which he retorted: Make me.

I did not make him. He showed Doreen his ear piercing, took her for a ride in his truck with its sleek chrome bumper and red rubber testicles hanging off the trailer hitch. Soon after, Doreen crumpled my notes in the recycle bin. They stretched each other's faces and laughed. I watched the whole opus and massacre from my office mail slot.

They married. She's out on maternity. The office threw a baby shower. I called in sick, returned to a stale piece of cake with ATIONS! in frosting. After the trucks depart, Clint faxes me: *How long have you been peeking in our windows? I heard you weeping in the landscaping. You woke her up. Don't think I don't notice you and that gay terrarium.*

I shouldn't think it's meaningful that I woke her, but I do.

In an Excel spreadsheet I compile reasons why I'm better than Clint to maybe give Doreen someday. I update it with: *Does not use "gay" flippantly.* Maybe I should buy a dog. Or take another trip. I fax the Intake Order Receipt and Transport Discharge to Archives.

Doreen's replacement, Jeff, likes that kind of high-five where he interlocks his fingers with yours so that you end up just standing there, holding hands over your heads like a couple of celebrating marathoners. But I don't have the nerve to let go.

The epidermises always arrive bundled in twine like hay bales, or so Larson says at lunch when we go over the Lab Harvest Review. I advise him, pale and choked up: TMI! To which he gulps and says, "Sorry, I forgot! How is Mr. Padula holding up?"

"How do you think?" I gasp.

"I don't know how you go on after something like that," he says, "your family just smashed into mush."

I twitch and say, "Show some respect. They were people. We ate Sunday dinner together. I went to his daughter's graduation party, for Christ's."

"You still racking yourself over that?" he says. "It was probably a deer, Randy. Deer are always causing wrecks on the interstate. I think maybe you should just talk to somebody. You know, about the hypothesis you're hypothesizing?" Larson coughs and then adds, "Of course, maybe you shouldn't, concerning the potential legalities and all."

After lunch I advise Prototypes: Develop lipstick #4217b, #4217c, and #4218a from collagen harvest NW-202. Samples ship to Marketing, where #4217b becomes Sunset Yore, #4217c Antebellum Blush, and #4218a Nude Fruit, which I'll learn in a faxed memorandum, while Larson down in Clinical Trials tests the products for safety.

At the end of the day, my intercom buzzes. It's Dengle.

"I'm evaluating internally for the new VP, you know," he says.

"I got the memo," I say.

"I'm winking into the intercom," he says. "I'm looking forward to the new autumn line."

*   *   *

At home, Mr. Padula has displayed the remaining sixteen bikes in his yard: tricycles to training-wheeled juniors to the full-size kind with multiple speeds. Some have handlebar tassels or pegs. A bicycle built for five. The sixteenth sits kickstanded beside him – the banana seat and side mirrors, a basket cradling the sign: FOR SALE.

His therapist suggested a lawn sale on the one-year anniversary of the crash. The bikes are baby steps. I've seen him through his window, cradling one of his wife's brushes in his palms, wheezing and rocking. Or chewing Cam and BJ's Legos. Or paper-cutting himself between his fingers with Natalie's high school diploma.

Mr. Padula smokes in a lawn chair, a cup of coffee Pisa-ing in the grass.

"How are things?" I say, sliding my wedding band off and on.

"Oh, you know," he says and shrugs.

"Any offers today?"

"Oh, you know," he says, turning his hand side to side.

I microwave leftovers, do push-ups during commercials. On the map I guesstimate the distance to the Grand Canyon: about eighty thumbs away. The VP promotion could punch my first plane ticket. Maybe I'll go to Pisa, or Hawaii and see a volcano. I could bring Doreen back a necklace made of obsidian. Bet assholing Clint never did that.

Outside, the mulch has soured during dusk, flaring the righteous pathetic out of my nostrils. I do a little bit of weeding while it's cool. I find a snapped rubber band caught on a root. Mr. Padula used to make these wooden rubber band guns with clothespin triggers. Rubber bands dangled in the rhododendrons between our yards. Once, one glistened slick with dew, hanging off the mailbox flag like a gallowed night crawler. I wonder how many might be hiding in the soil had his family not slammed into that overpass.

"You know what?" I say to Mr. Padula. "I forgot. A coworker is having his nephew stay with him for a week. He wanted me to get him a bike."

Mr. Padula rubs his face, his thick eyebrows up as he looks at the rows. "Which one?"

I shrug and tap my toe in the dirt.

Mr. Padula paces the bikes, settling on a junior one. He grips the handlebars, runs his hand over the frame, pats the seat. "How about this? This okay? Is the nephew still – ?" he says and holds his hand above the ground, which means to ask if the nephew is about four-foot, still little, around his twins', BJ and Cam's, heights.

"That should do," I say, rubbing my neck and blinkblinkblinking. "How much?"

"Jeez," he says, scratching his head. "Five bucks?"

"Here's ten," I say. "My coworker gave me a ten."

Mr. Padula holds the bill between his trembling hands. "I don't got change," he says. "I can't make change." He looks at the rows of bikes again, moving his jaw side to side. "Maybe he should take another bike then. Maybe take one of them trikes?"

"I don't think he needs a tricycle," I say.

"Aw, hell, take it," Mr. Padula sniffles, shoving it my way.

I load them into my car, watch him shrink in the rearview as he wheels the bikes back into his garage full of cardboard boxes. Dusk pales and periwinkles, the clouds converge and bruise, and everything is brushstroked with the suggestion of smoldering.

Six miles outside town, past the orchard, is the dirt road to the defunct limestone quarry.

Utica Quarry is a dozen football fields in size. The county's converting it into a reservoir. Part of the road is flooded. The only way down is to rappel the twenty-foot benches. Dad was a backhoe operator here. He griped about befouling the karst and accumulations of calcium carbonate. "The stuff's damn insoluble," he'd grunt, hiking up special socks over varicose veins that bulged from his calves like embossed trees.

When he died, the doctor said his liver was firm and stratumed with deposits.

I push the bikes to the edge of the first bench and toss them in. They fall twenty feet to the next bench, clunking atop all the other bikes. Wheels spin, baseball cards flap in the spokes. I cry until they quiet, say another prayer, then head home.

*   *   *

Later in the week is Developmental Briefings with Dengle. Fragrance introduces Enamor™, Cuticles presents a line of nail polishes called Heirlooms™. Moisturizers is absent. A shipment of mink fat came in and Perez had to advise: Prep to intake and initiate mink oil extraction. I present Dixie Charms™: Sunset Yore, Antebellum Blush, and Nude Fruit.

Dengle winks, which I take to mean: *Expectations exceeded.* I think my first order of business as VP will be to fire Clint, or maybe demote him to placenta collection. I'll promote Doreen to my assistant and take her to lunch in the bird atrium gazebo and tell her how much I like her working beneath me. Though that might be sexual harassment.

Dengle was impressed with my Yummys!™ flavored lip glosses. He said strawberry rhubarb was just like Grandma used to make. I've been on his radar ever since. The Yummys!™ line replaced Retro Chic™, which included an absorbent collagen booster that increased voluptuousness by 65 percent, and a protein enzyme harvested from the Clostridium botulinum bacteria to reduce oral commissure wrinkles.

Except Clinical Trials found that the Clostridium botulinum produced a mild neurotoxin. Lick your lips enough and the headaches started, the blurry vision, the light sensitivity. Maybe a hand numbed or a leg spasmed or a body seizured. So the report said. Larson said if just one person gets even the mildest sniffle, Clinical Trials is required to list it as a side effect because of legalities. After the Padula car wreck, I scrapped the line, shredded the files, and went on a week-long bender to Niagara Falls where I was pulled back from the fence by a tour guide when he caught me trying to jump in.

The leafy green hue of Niagara was from the rock flour, which Dad explained was pulverized mineral dust. Utica was full of it. I remember him coughing up quarry and swallowing it back down. It caked in his nostrils and mustache.

The last person to present is Clint. He offers Bimini™, a new Botox with 85 percent more pull and includes a formula for cell renewal, increased lipid barrier function, and elasticity. "Look," he says, squinting. Except no crow's feet or parenthetical wrinkles form. His face moves but it doesn't. It's sort of terrifying and brilliant.

Dengle stands, applauding: *Bravo! Bravo! Bravo!*

Later I shred the memorandum announcing Clint as the new VP.

*   *   *

I detour on Route 365. I see a bunch of fish heads nailed to the side of a barn. At home I trace the new route on the map in red. Slowly, Upstate New York is looking like a cardiovascular system. Except I don't know where the heart is. Maybe it's Albany.

Mr. Padula sits in his yard with the fourteen remaining bikes, practicing his wave and small talk for the part-time work he puts in as a Walmart greeter some weekends. A few kids play roller hockey in the street and he tries not to watch them.

His family had been returning from Sand Plains State Park. His oldest, Natalie, placed twenty-fifth in a triathlon there. She was studying biology at Syracuse. During vacations she would rummage through my trash for the recyclables I didn't separate. His identical twins, BJ and Cam, would take the recyclables and set up racecourses in the street for their bikes, and when the bikes got bigger with them, they started bunny-hopping stacks of cans. They'd brought their sleds to Sand Plains to race down the dunes. It was presumed by the median ruts crossing I-90 that Mrs. Padula lost control. Mr. Padula asked me to go to the hospital with him, pickled drunk. Tara was coming home later and later then, smelling of Italian. Under those sheets like that. All that skin. It wasn't something we should've seen. The hospital returned a baggie of belongings. An earring, a Game Boy button, a nickel, a prototype tube of Retro Chic™ I'd snuck to Mrs. Padula. They found it wedged in a dash vent.

"All the hot stuffs today," Mrs. Padula would joke, puckering her lips. "I need help!"

But she was not unattractive. She had a pencil-eraser mole on her temple, which she concealed with graying bangs. Mr. Padula refused to let her remove it. I could've made a million off bottling the glow she got when talking about her kids, her husband.

They can't even autopsy, I overheard a nurse say. *Where would you begin?*

I went to the overpass once. The median ruts were mud-puddled and rippling with mosquitoes. I looked for hoof tracks. The crack in the concrete pylon began thick at my waist, forking and tapering upward into thin slivers. There was a wilted bouquet jutting from the thick part of the crack. I was sobbing and snotting down my face.

Mr. Padula practices his greeting and wave as crickets purr throughout his lawn. He says the work is about keeping busy, not the money. I see it as a thwarting. To counterbalance the leaving with as many welcomes as he can accumulate.

My eye spasms so hard it's like the right side of my face avalanches.

Did Mrs. Padula lick her lips a lot? is all I've wanted to ask him for eleven months.

Instead, I buy another bike. "For a corporate charity auction," I tell him.

I toss it into the quarry. I consider peeking in Doreen's window. Maybe right now Doreen is knitting baby booties or rubbing Belle® lotion on her round belly to reduce stretch marks. But Clint's truck is in the driveway, those big red rubber hitch testes fuck-youing me. So I settle for slowing, trying to look in the lit windows as I pass.

*   *   *

"We've got a precarious situation on our hands," Dengle says. "I won't say it. You both received the memo. Speaking about the situation may only solidify it as a genuine hanger-on issue. Maybe *solidify* was a poor choice. I've said too much."

It's just me and Clint in Dengle's office. The door is closed.

But the memorandum only said: *Urgent.*

So Dengle elaborates. Seven of the ten Bimini™ rats are dead. The rest have unquenchable thirst, sated only if they aren't too confused to locate the water bottle. Fevers are running high to delirium. One of the five group testers is comatose.

"Why is Randolph here?" Clint says. He furrows except he doesn't. His forehead moves in one smooth sheet. No striae at the eye corners. His cheeks rise and his eyelids lower, which means he's squinting, which means either *upset* or *confused*.

"Because he's got expertise," Dengle says.

"I do?" I say.

Dengle frowns. "Don't be coy. Are you my ex-wife? Do you fail to reduce the sodium-content of your cooking and clip your toenails in bed to provoke me?"

I shake my head.

"Then don't be coy," Dengle says. "I know about the hiccup with Retro Chic™."

"The hiccup?"

He rolls his eyes. "What did I just say about being coy? I know about the Padulas. You're just lucky there wasn't an autopsy. You know it's frowned upon to distribute prototype products, Randolph. You want the competition one-upping us?"

Larson, I think, hot-eared, *that assholing spineless finking gossipy nutsack.*

"What's worse than a bridesmaid?" Dengle asks. "The press gets wind of the coma and we'll be the, the, the groom's-drunk-racist-uncle-who-makes-a-scene-and-maybe-hits-on-the-bride's-mother-or-fondles-her-tit to Maybelline!"

Dengle makes air-quotes. "Aka downsizing and layoffs."

"Nothing is wrong with the injections! Look!" Clint declares and shoots up his face. He sticks the hypodermic needle into the corrugator muscles several times. Little bubbles rise under his skin, little droplets of red bloom. The bumps flatten, the blood dries, and his brow lifts as if he's surprised, his face unfolding like a song.

"I think we should scrap the line and pay the tester's medical expenses," I say.

"If I wanted ship-jumping I'd have videoconferenced my ex-wife," Dengle says. "Ship-jumping will not get us to Maybelline bride status."

Clint pales, his neck sweats, and he clears his throat a few times.

I request, "Clarify my expertise?"

To which Dengle replies, "What did you do for Mr. Padula? You pay him hush?"

My eye goes twitch, twitch, twitch, and I imagine jumping out his twelfth-story window.

Dengle takes the *twitch twitch twitch* to mean *wink wink wink*, and he winks three times in return, which I take to mean, *Understood, hush it is.*

"Maybe we should phone Miller in PR," Clint says, not noticing the exchange.

"If I wanted naysaying, you know who I would have phoned?" Dengle says.

*   *   *

The week passes. I continue developing Dixie Charms™, circum-navigating the fringe of what could be my Albany, my blink tic curling half of my face into a fist. I buy more bikes from Mr. Padula. "Next month's a year," he says. "The missus was a packrat. You seen the garage? Kept everything. The baby clothes and toys and Walkmans and science projects. The house is a freaking museum." He sort of statics after saying that.

His therapist suggested he use the lawn sale money to buy an "in memoriam."

"What's an in memoriam?" I ask.

"A plaque or statue or garden or scholarship fund in their name," he says and shrugs.

I spin my wedding band, wondering if it's more an in memoriam or a memorandum.

"You're going to sell everything?" I ask.

He inhales deeply. "I suppose. Guess I should get to the bank so I can make change."

"How'd you do it?" I ask. "How'd you make peace with it?"

An ice cream truck jingles and turns down our street. Mr. Padula sticks his fingers in his ears and shuts his eyes until it passes. Then he runs his fingers through some handlebar tassels. "I didn't say I did," he says. "How am I supposed to do that?"

Mr. Padula squints at me, "That spasm is getting worse. Might want to see a doctor."

"It's been a tough year," I say, tears flicking off my jerking face.

Mr. Padula doesn't notice, or maybe he doesn't care, because tears are on his cheeks, too.

"Preaching to the choir," he tells me.

*   *   *

I can't sleep. I sweat into the sheets. I toss to Tara's side, roll over, and face the wall where the bicycle-built-for-five leans. If I drift off, I imagine Mrs. Padula applying Retro Chic™ in the dark rearview, Natalie sleeping in the passenger seat with dried sweat salt on her cheeks, the twins passing a Game Boy between them, faces aglow in the screen. Then Mrs. Padula's arm slumps, or her foot spasms into the accelerator, or she starts to tremble and foam at the mouth. Or maybe everything is fine and a goddamn deer comes out of nowhere.

Next time I toss, I'm driving to Utica, the windows fogging faster than I can defrost them. I want to throw myself into the quarry. Night crawlers on the road make parts of themselves fat then thin, wriggling and undulating like a living signature.

Up the dirt road is a truck with red rubber testicles hanging off the trailer hitch.

A rope is tied to the hitch. It falls over the first couple of quarry benches. I hear a thin clinking and grunting echo out of the pit. On the third bench, just above where the reservoir floodwaters have risen and reflect a gibbous moon, is someone chipping at the escarpment with a pickax, filing down the little limestone chunks over a bucket.

In the truck bed is a statue: a person sleeping, dressed in a hospital gown. The hair looks like brown coral, the fingernails shiny quartz. I tap the skull and it feels like stone I haven't felt before. It sort of gives a little without breaking.

From the mouth comes a cough, a cloud of white dust, and I run for the bushes.

Out of the quarry, the figure drags the statue from the truck and pushes it over each bench precipice until it's sunk in the floodwater, bubbling and rippling the moonlight. I run up the trail back to my car. At home I shiver under the covers, watching the light creep up the walls and the clock hands tick until the alarm goes off and it's Monday morning.

*   *   *

Before the first shipment of epidermises arrives, I elevator down to B3's Tuscarora Clinic. I find the botulinum #2146d cage. The rat ear-tagged *92f* gasps on the wheel. Rat *92j* pants a bloody tongue. Rat *92m* sleeps on its side, except without breathing. It sinks into the sawdust bedding. Stitched into its side meat I see patches of crystallized white mica. Its tongue, a stiff fossil. Its teeth, stalactited and stalagmited.

Beside botulinum #2146d are cages labeled botulinum #2146d.1, #2146d.2, and #2146d.3. These rats look okay, eating pellets and sucking from the water bottle, except for the occasional eye-rolling and coughing and swallowing.

I elevator up to Rejuvenation, march into Clint's office without knocking. He's tying off his arm, holding a syringe, which he explains, with the rubber tube ends between his teeth, is an electrolyte supplement for the dehydration. He's thin, pasty, perfect, minus the dead skin flaking from his temples. I inform him about the petrified rat. He frowns. "You should see the insides," he says, shaking his head. "The insides look like pumice."

"It's the calcium," I tell him. "I saw you at the quarry."

"Calcium's important to protect the lipid barrier. For skin regeneration."

"Not if it's in your blood," I say.

"Like you would know," he says, rolling his eyes, and I swear it sounds like gravel.

My breath stutters. "Like you could know how I know?"

"Thing is," Clint says, his thick forearm veins bulging. "Thing is?" He pants and his tongue is all mica-crystal-patchwork-bloody. "Thing is, Rudolph. Is – is – is you don't persist. You're a quitter. Which is why you are the VP and I am not. Why is Doorknob my lovely Doreen is my lovely Doreen and yours is not? Maybe she's born with it?"

"Think of her," I say, and do, maybe Tara. "You're going to be a dad."

"Twins. Not so good. What I do I do because."

"You didn't give her Bimini™ did you?" I ask.

"You fucking my therapist?" Clint says, and pisses himself. Then he keels over.

*   *   *

Except he doesn't keel, but comas, turns out.

Medics carry him to an ambulance while one squeezes a hand-held ventilator balloon strapped to his mouth. They look into his eyes with a penlight. His pupils do not contract. The whites look marbled, quartzed, dolomited, Triassic.

I elevator to the top floor where the glass walls overlook the east side of town, a sliver of traffic, and the latticework of power lines that reach across the lush green like skeletons Red Rovering. Dengle has his feet on the desk. I advise: Terminate Bimini™!

But Dengle shakes his head, "Not even Clinique has a lipid-barrier rejuvenator," he says, "much less Maybelline. Utica is our thick-peckered *groom*." When I refer him back to the snafus re: the drunk-uncle-tit-fondler-to-the-bride, he stretches casually. "Taken care of. Thanks to your expertise," he says, and throws me winks and elbow nudges.

My eye goes twitch twitch twitch.

"Exactly," he says. "This is why we have trials, Randolph. To troubleshoot."

"But at what cost?" I say. "What about Clint?"

Dengle sighs. "I think you're familiar with the cracking-eggs-omelet metaphor?"

"This is perverse," I say.

"No, it's beauty," Dengle says. "Beauty is intended to please a moral sensibility. Moral sensibility is based on tradition. The Chinese bind feet, Ethiopians insert lip plates, the Burmese wear brass rings to elongate necks to sheer elegance, and in America, here in New York, we tattoo, augment breasts, pierce, stretch faces. It wouldn't be beauty if everyone agreed with it. It wouldn't be tradition. It'd just be general consensus."

He cracks his knuckles. "One person's immorality is another person's beauty."

It's true. Even with all the Belle® eye cream the tic is sinking me fast.

Maybe a bird flies into the window with a thud. We turn and look at nothing together.

"And," he says, "I can out your skeleton to Mr. Padula."

To which I inquire, "What about the omelet?"

To which he informs me, "I'll crack the dozen to save the carton."

So I take hush and severance, box my possessions in the terrarium, feeling a black callused hitchhiking thumb of a terrible. I imagine Clint sunk into Utica, or deposited in the Upstate landscape, some sediment of the panoramic sentiment. I think of Tara and the Italian, their collective suffixed vowels, the lines on their map if they do such a pathetic thing. They share spaghetti, their lips meet, and I puke into my trash can.

Larson's at the vending machine as I'm leaving. I wrestle him down and punch.

"I'm sorry!" he cries, shielding himself. "I'm sorry I told!"

I keep punching him until security yanks me off and escorts me out of the building.

* * *

Unemployed and twitching, I attempt geomantic rearrangements of my furniture, trying to achieve something I read about in a magazine called *feng shui,* hoping I can harmonize my *chi* and channel heaven so that I can ask Mrs. Padula, "Was it a deer?"

After socking Larson, I have my swollen hand looked at, and seeing my tic, the doctor prescribes me something called alprazolam. The blinking slows and I assume *chi,* a tightness in my chest I didn't even know was there until I feel it evaporate. Breezes feel like blown kisses. I kiss back. I sit in a chair and maybe two weeks pass. Then I read the possible side effects and discontinue treatment, driving up and down I-90, sobbing sorry sorry sorry at the overpass crack. I throw out every Belle® product in meek protest and dry out, dandruff, raccoon-face, wrinkle, blemish, halitosis, hangnail, crack, peel, sag, and discolor.

With the severance and hush I research Hawaii and imagine throwing myself into a lava hole. Then the Italian is in the lava hole. Then I'm on a palm-treed beach, rubbing coconut oil onto Tara, or Doreen's big stomach. *They can call me Daddy,* I say. *They don't have to know. Blood relation, schmlud relation.* I visualize a feng shuied bamboo porch, a twin in each arm, maybe Clint-like ear piercings out of respect, Doreen inside baking pies and coming out with floury hands to watch me sing them to sleep, and I *chi* all over the place. I book two tickets to Hawaii, telling myself: *Jerk Jerk Jerk* and *But? But? But?*

At Utica I tie a rope to a tree, rappel down to the first bench, and retrieve two tricycles.

Clint's truck is in the driveway but I know he's not home. I park down the street. I almost ring the doorbell. Then I get down on one knee and almost ring the doorbell. Then I put the Hawaii tickets in my teeth and almost ring the doorbell. Then I leave the tricycles on the stoop and ring the doorbell and hide in the landscaping.

She opens the door. Her eyes red and wet and swollen. Her stomach is a fine basin under her dress. Her lips full and fat. Her scalene nose is equilateraled and streamlined. This is Doreen but also not. This is Tara but also not. Her forehead wrinkles are gone.

She sees the tricycles and her face moves but it doesn't.

The thing about full lips is that they are a subliminal indication of fertility and drive men bananas via primordial need. Full lips excite our "caveman instinct." This was the beginning of my presentation for Retro Chic™. Of course, the irony is that men and women who use collagen and Botox do so to inflate the perception of what is not there.

I just watch her snot down her face and touch her tummy and cry cry cry.

If beauty is to please a moral sensibility and I am here in these bushes no longer finding Doreen beautiful because of this primordial need awareness, or some guilt or shame or fear that she won't love me back, or if I ever loved her, or she will and it means it's truly over with Tara, I wonder what it is I find beautiful. What is moral and right to me?

Clint was wrong about me being a quitter. I don't know when to quit is the problem.

Doreen looks up and down the street then shuts the door, leaving the trikes on the stoop.

*   *   *

The doorbell rings some Saturday and my head is throbbing and splitting. I took a few Xanax with wine and woke up naked with morning wood and a belt around my neck, lying in the tub with the toaster. I remember seeing the newspaper headline. Doreen had given birth: these two little silted figurines, gorgeous and horrified and still.

I put on some pants, pop an aspirin, and open the door. It's Mr. Padula.

"You got change?" he says. "I forgot to get to the bank."

His yard is full of people browsing the cardboard boxes from his garage.

I've been grieving a zit for days and feel a soreness swell. I press it, worried that the soreness only goes so far inward. I hope it can go deeper than that. Odd to hope there is more of me that can still be hurt.

I feel Mr. Padula's stare but can't meet it. I tear up and start to snot bubble.

"I'm sorry," I say. "I can't make change either."

Mr. Padula touches my shoulder, "Hey, hey. It's all right. I'll just switch the price. Don't bang yourself up about it. Why're you banging yourself up? I know what you've been doing with them bikes. I appreciate it. But you can't do everything."

I nod.

"Yeah," he says and sidesteps his slumping spine between the rhododendrons.

I clean up in the mirror. My shoulders are dandruffed, belt marks chafe my throat. My face spasms, tired, weathered, pocked, and porous. Mr. Padula is maybe twice as old as me. But I look worse in half the time. Excavated, unexfoliated, this is me.

And it's terrifying. To think someone would let themselves live this way.

The crowd rummages through cardboard boxes labeled: TOYS, CLOTHES, TROPHIES. A sign out front reads: NAME YOUR PRICE, EVERYTHING MUST GO. I take my wedding band off and put it in the jewelry box that a woman is perusing. Another woman pays

Mr. Padula ten bucks for three baby strollers and loads them into her minivan. Somebody else is checking out the patterns on the bedspreads. A woman directs her son to take an entire box of VHS tapes. The son has padlocks hanging from his pierced ears, and he wears a KwikStop uniform with the nametag: HELLO MY NAME IS BERNIE.

I browse boxes until I come across a chessboard and bag of ceramic pieces.

"That's Cam's," Mr. Padula says. "We played every week."

I hold a piece, heavy and cold in my hand.

"The board's walnut and maple," Mr. Padula says. "Made it in my wood shop class." He picks up a castle turret, a pawn, both with creepy anthropomorphic faces. "I kiln-fired these from a mold in the ceramics class I taught at the high school."

He examines a bishop with a broken face. "Could take five for all of it."

I advise: Do not sell this.

To which he says, "But everything is supposed to go."

He scrunches, unfurling wrinkles across his face that mean something, have good reason.

"Why don't you keep it and we'll play?" I offer.

Mr. Padula turns a piece in his hand. "Every week?"

"Sure," I tell him. "It'll be our own tradition."

"You any good?" he asks, eyebrows up.

"I don't know how to play," I find myself lying.

"Well, here," he says, "jeez." He turns over an empty box and sets up the board. We sit in the grass and he points to pieces. "This is the king. He's the one you want to capture. That's called *checkmate*. This is the queen. She can move anywhere on the board. Do you know what this piece is called?" he asks, holding up a horse.

"The pony?" I say.

"It's called a knight," Mr. Padula says with a chuckle. It's the first time I remember him laughing in a long time, and I laugh at that, or me, or us sitting here, unable to recall the last time I laughed too, and some of that tightness and tic in me lifts.

We play, pausing whenever he makes a sale. The sun moves across the sky, shifting the skirts of shadows around the pieces. I make intentional bad moves. Sometimes I take one of his pieces and Mr. Padula laughs. "Good! Good! You're learning!" Boxes empty, the crowd thins. The ice cream truck comes and goes and he doesn't even notice.

Mr. Padula has me in a third checkmate when some neighborhood kid shows up.

He's holding the science fair project volcano, and Mr. Padula gives it to him for free. Then he brings out kitchen supplies and tells the kid to fill the conduit with baking soda and add vinegar to the crater. The kid does. The volcano erupts.

"How'd you do that?" the kid says.

"I did most of them projects," Mr. Padula says, nodding to the box with the solar system, the digestive tract, the dinosaurs. He cites facts he learned with his children as they worked. "You know the small intestines is like twenty-three feet long?" He mentions the Oort cloud, how dinosaurs became birds, then the thing about erosion that I don't believe.

"Look it up," he says, handing me the *N* encyclopedia from a box.

I do, and he's right.

The current rate of erosion for Niagara Falls is approximately one foot per year.

"A whole foot?" I say. "It's lost twenty-nine feet since I've been born."

Mr. Padula takes a large tape measure from his toolbox and hands me the end. We back away from each other twenty-nine feet, a good width of his yard. The boy puts his hand on the tape at eleven feet to stake his claim in the footage of damage. Then Mr. Padula tells me to keep backing up, and I sidestep the rhododendrons into my yard until he yells, "Stop." We're a good distance apart now. "I'm fifty-eight," he shouts to me. "This is what's happened in my life."

We stand like that for a long time, considering it.

My Kind of Utmost Tender

Each week at Pogz, me and Duane Duane attend a thematic Monday Midday Meeting. Beats me why we don't utilize the MMM concepts. Duane Duane refuses to compromise his quote-unquote "creative intellect." I'm just a creature of habit. So sue me.

This week's MMM theme is DAMP: Developing an Affordable, Marketable Product.

Excerpt:

HR Pete (passive and protocoled): So how might we make our product more affordable?

Me (standing; I currently don't sit and sleep only on my stomach): Lower prices?

HR Pete: I guess let's maybe only yield constructive proposals if possible, please?

Duane Duane (scratching his head bandana): Construct pogs from recycled cardboard?

Me (rolling my eyes): Construct slammers from recycled aluminum cans?

HR Pete: Let's recall that funds are presently insufficient for such a redesign? However, I do acknowledge your economical thought processes and will continue to encourage such in the coming fiscal quarters even if they are currently, and remain, unfeasible.

Me: So maybe we should make funds sufficient then?

HR Pete (wincing): Sorry, but DAMP-irrelevant? Paul, I'm requesting you please sit?

I respectfully decline and rub a lumbar disc like it's herniated. But it's fine. I lie.

HR Pete: What about marketability? Paul, your standing is borderline distracting?

Duane Duane (making a lens frame with his hands): Maybe commercials?

HR Pete: So I guess I'm going to also stand. In all honesty, I'm uncomfortable and intimidated with Paul's almost towering. I'm unclear on what's protocol here. I'm sorry but I guess I'm going to have to bite the bullet and be the bad guy on this one and put my foot down and pull the trigger, so to speak, and say standing is no longer an option in all future meetings. Unless it's the Friday Pep, of course, and in that case *sitting* isn't an option. I'll type up an office policy and distribute the memo via the email Listserv. While I'm up I guess I could stretch for my indoor soccer game. I've had this nagging crick in my shin . . .

Me: Maybe we can make recyclable advertisements?

Duane Duane (slapping my back, thumbs upped): That's good stuff, Paul!

HR Pete, with one foot on the conference table, stops reaching for his toes to look at me like I must be joking. I am but I'm also not.

Then HR Pete distributes the post-MMM Efficiency Assessment. Question A: *Please use the provided space to suggest comments/ideas on how we might make MMMs more productive.* Question B: *Please use the provided space to suggest comments/ideas on how we might make Efficiency Assessments (EFFAs) more productive in making MMMs more productive.*

Duane Duane fills his EFFA's provided space with sketches of slammers, which drives HR Pete bonkers because it's not protocol. HR Pete requests he use the proposal form. Duane Duane is an artist. He's got a vision. I'm just a random corking hobbyist. I've got a tangible skeleton in my closet. I waddle like a penguin. I write in my

EFFA's provided space: *Eliminate the EFFA.* Later the standard reply email will come from HR Pete: *Thanks for your great input! Together we'll make Pogz a leader in the gaming industry!*

Note to self: On the next EFFA maybe write: *Fire HR Pete.*

After the MMM and EFFA adjourn, me and Duane Duane Rock-Paper-Scissors for mail duty. We're the primary staff, just us two. CEO Kiffin fishes on the lake all day with his Golden Parachute while we hustle around the rented office space above the nearly twister-demolished Bowl-O-Drome. He leaves all dealings to HR Pete, coming in only when necessary, pulsing the windowpanes with the throttled growls of his red chopper, mock casting and reeling in me or Duane Duane, reeking of cheap plastic-bottle gin, and fashioning a five o'clock shadow that must be the ghost of his former ambition. Bet he kisses the plastic gin bottle as much as his two ankle-biters and wife, Mrs. Kiffin, VP, who arrives the earliest to collect CEO Kiffin's mail. She's pretty in a rotund way, with these sharp cheekbones all done-up, permed and stockingless. Duane Duane's two cents about her, elbow-nudging me and winking: She's the early bird catching worm. She leads a wake of perfume like scented tears, probably to battle the stench of plastic-bottle gin. She collects the mail on his enormous oak desk left by me or Duane Duane depending on how poorly one of us selects Rock or Paper or Scissors.

Her perfume is tragic for good reason. Commitment is something like the carotid or the jugular. Beats me why anyone would want to show it. Beats me why anyone would volunteer to be utmost tender. Not my kind of utmost tender. The emotional kind.

Duane Duane Papers. I regrettably Rock.

He covers my fist, gives a thumbs-up and victorious howl. I recall Moxy.

Last winter I let my terrier, Moxy, out to pee before work, and a municipal plow compacted her into a snowbank. She was my fluffy white confidant, no fink. Poor thing never stood a chance. Spring thaw, I buried her. Duane Duane bugged me at work, asking, Why so mopey? Finally, I told him. He slapped my back and gave a mournful thumbs-down. He offered to buy me a beer so we could honor her right. Bereft, I said sure.

Me: How do you spell your name? I'll look you up in the white pages.

Him: D-U-A-N-E. Duane.

Me (rolling my eyes): Your last name, genius.

We just stared at each other for a while. We never got that beer.

As I waddle to Postal, I stop by Reception and ask Admin Gwynn if I received any messages while attending the MMM or EFFA. I'm waiting for a very important call.

Admin Gwynn (biting a fake red fingernail of decent back-scratching length): Nope.

She flutters wispy lashes and asks if I did something different with my hair. What I did was spray on brown because I ran out of Saharan Dune blond.

Note to self: Everything should come canned. Success, Courage, Companionship.

Me to her: Literally had my ears lowered.

Admin Gwynn giggles and then grabs my Dynamo! tie, pulling me close. I smell her herbal shampoo and minty blemish cream. My lifegiver maybe flinches. I'm careful of my posture. Her teeth are a good biting white. Her nose has a deviated septum, so it whistles like a songbird. I tap my foot to her exhaled tune.

Her (admiring my Dynamo! tie): That's so *hawt!*

It's not hot. I know what she's doing and I let her. It's innocent enough. So sue me. But I can't noodle her. I'm currently clandestine and corked. Plus, I'm short one paper bag. Plus, there is an office policy on liaisons. I could get slammed.

By *slammed,* I mean *fired.*

Dynamo! was CEO Kiffin's popular '80s Cold War board game. The player/superpower to put the first man on the moon and harvest the most nuclear weapons wins. Me and Duane Duane dust it off whenever we get sick of beta testing pogs.

Admin Gwynn puts her mouth to my ear, says she's tired of the cat and mouse. She asks, Do I want to meet her in the Postal cubicle after work and watch her bald kitty eat a yo-yo? My lifegiver definitely flinches. Her nose sirens. Her breath, teasing sweet. What is protocol here? I should be appalled. I'm more curious in an anatomically viable kind of way.

Me (shrugging): Sure.

Then I waddle to Postal.

When the Cold War ended so did Dynamo! CEO Kiffin failed to imitate his success with xtreme: Rock-Paper-Scissors after its recall due to lawsuits involving plaintiffs bandaged and stabbed and concussed. Then he developed rectangular mats for Rochambeau?!, which harsh criticisms of I bet drove him to the coniferous taste of plastic-bottle gin. He finally rallied with Pogz in the early '90s when I was just a boy. Now I'm cusping thirty. Modern entertainment is almost entirely digital. Pogs have become nostalgic and rudimentary. We've wasted multiple MMMs brainstorming, putting ourselves in the clientele's shoes, solving WIIFMs? *What's In It For Me?* we ask. But nothing is in it for anybody. Pogs were once collectible. Now they're trivial and forgotten.

In Postal, I sort the incoming, lick stamps for outgoing. I don't sit. I deliver to the HR cubicle. I drop a bundle of fishing mags on CEO Kiffin's oak desk, which reeks of disinfectant spray. Beside the wastebasket sits a balled-up beige stocking. A nearby floor vent announces the thunderous clatter of bowling pins below.

Near the Production cubicle, Admin Gwynn finds me. She tells me she just transferred a call to my voicemail. She winks, mimics yo-yo tricks and says it appears somebody has photocopied her fanny. There is a fanny imprint on the copier glass.

But I'm not up for the cat and mouse.

I detour back to Postal and check voicemail. It's MD Kowalski over at Upstate Memorial General.

Him: The lightbulb needs to be surgically extracted, no ifs, ands, or *butts.*

MD Kowalski's medical humor is textbook punny. I'm scheduled for surgery tomorrow. I'm told not to clench because if it shatters we're talking all kidding aside.

I figured this much and shudder. Still, I'm glad for patient confidentiality.

Experimentation is a method of acquiring knowledge. Note to self: Some things that go in don't always come back out. Like a billiard ball in the mouth. It was self-inflicted, accidental. There is a lonely void in me that this fills. So sue me.

I delete the voicemail and deliver waning orders to Production, where we laminate pogs and use a toaster oven to melt pewter for the slammer molds. The toaster oven has a crack in the side as if it sustained tremendous weight. The fubared pog-cutter has its lid up, which is a safety hazard and violates office policy. When I go to close it, I notice a pog stuck to a circular blade. This is typical. Funds are too insufficient to resharpen the cutter. Sometimes things just get stuck. But the pog isn't familiar. It's a photograph of two naked people all pretzeled up and noodling. I cock my head. My lifegiver flinches as if to say, *Interested?*

Duane Duane must be on a special contract for a bachelor party. But I never got cc'ed on any Product Status Update. So I waddle to Design, the floor resonating through my bony calves from the pin resetting machines below. Stale cigar smoke and sweaty rental shoes waft from the floor vents. Currently we're completing Duane Duane's most recent authorized edition: Pandora's Pogz. Duane Duane designed the tsunami and bubonic plague pogs. I designed the volcano and oil spill pogs. They're packaged in a box, duh.

Duane Duane is watching old Rochambeau?! footage on the Internet, shaking his head with artistic offense. I know it's Rochambeau?! because I hear the sounds of two people groaning, nauseous. Over his shoulder, I see them listing on their sections of the rectangular mat as they alternate kicking each other in the lifegivers.

I show Duane Duane the pog and ask why I wasn't cc'ed on this PSU.

Duane Duane (snatching the pog away): You're not supposed to see that.

Me: Why not?

Duane Duane (stiffening): I can't say that I can say.

I'm quick to remind him how he nagged me about Moxy getting plowed.

Him (looking around, whispering): Fine. You can keep a secret, right?

I think: *Duh?*

Me (shrugging): Sure.

Him (tightening the bandana on his head): You promise?

Me (rolling my eyes): Yes.

Him (for serious): Don't roll your eyes at me, Paul. Say, *I promise.*

He opens his desk drawer and adds the pog to a tackle box full of similar ones. HR Pete must have authorized overtime. Every pog depicts the same two people noodling: in an executive leather chair, standing on mail bins, on a copy machine mid-copy.

Me (inspecting another pog): I promise. P-R-O-M-I-S-E. Promise.

Him: Don't patronize me. And quit the sarcasm.

But sarcasm is emotional Kevlar. So sue me.

Me (humoring him, for serious): Fine, I promise.

I notice the male noodler wears a bandana and gives hearty thumbs-ups.

Noodling proceeds on a toaster oven, on an enormous oak desk.

That's when I recognize the rotund female's cheekbones all done up.

And I clench, bewildered. I think something maybe shatters.

Duane Duane (responding to my bugged eyes): She's my muse. We're in love.

I cringe, choked, cautiously unclench.

Duane Duane tells me to calm down. If HR Pete hears me gasping or sees me this pale, he'll make us both fill out Medical Event Descriptions and Proclamations of Accident/Illness in Notations. He tells me that months ago, when my Rock beat his Scissors, he delivered CEO Kiffin's fishing mags and found Mrs. Kiffin, VP weeping at the oak desk. Duane Duane consoled her, gave her lacked, necessary attention. Simply, he was there. Made her feel integral, important. Her loneliness inspired him. She prefers ambition. He prefers unconventionally wide women. The kiss just happened. She told him to come to Pogz an hour early the next day. He brought chocolates and wore loose-fitting pants. She let him in.

The rest: etc. etc. etc.

I wiggle and feel the bulb intact. I sigh, relieved.

I find a pog where Duane Duane is nude and cuffed to the radiator behind Admin Gwynn's desk while Mrs. Kiffin, VP spanks him with a blue Swingline.

I waddle to my desk and drop my blue stapler into the trash with a tissue.

I think of CEO Kiffin alone on the lake, crisp marigold dawn breaking across the palisades where a boy jumped and collided with a passing boat and was never found. CEO Kiffin, gin-pickled, concerning himself with the fishing line's nervous tug while Mrs. Kiffin,

VP intricately positions herself for grunting sweating Duane Duane here at Pogz. Her face on the pog terrifies me. The intimate face is the ultimate fink.

And I wonder what it takes to risk the hurt that might come from opening up to another. Is it really worth the possible humiliation? What if I offer myself to someone who rejects the real me? So instead I temporarily fill my void with the delicate knack of random corking behind closed curtains, only occasionally negotiating an affair via kinky Internet chats. We'll rendezvous at the Midnite Majestic Motel, drink boxed wine, listen to the night wind howl and swirl, and decorate a paper bag with glitter and markers and yarn. I wear that paper bag over my finking face while we noodle. So sue me.

On another pog, Duane Duane shaves Mrs. Kiffin, VP's calves as she sits on the enormous oak desk, tossing her balled-up beige stockings into the wastebasket.

I recall the disinfectant spray, consider the sanctity of marriage and really grieve it.

Me: But CEO Kiffin is going to frigging slam you.

By *slam* I mean *pummel.* Or *fire.* Or both, I guess.

Duane Duane (shaking his head): We're eloping. And you promised, right?

Eventually, in will stagger CEO Kiffin, burned and peeling from reflected lake sunlight, to collect his piling mail. Mrs. Kiffin, VP will be long gone, untitled, maiden-named, or Duaned. The ribald pogs will be on the desk. Bet the desk will flare up from all the disinfectant spray, a brilliant blue flame. The tackle box of pogs is metaphorical. How Mrs. Kiffin, VP should feel but is trapped inside CEO Kiffin's true love and priority.

Duane Duane says they'll probably go someplace meek and arid, like Utah. He's got full creative control of his new partnership with Mrs. Kiffin, VP: a modernized digital Chutes & Ladders spinoff: Escalators & Elevators.

Me: What about CEO Kiffin's two boys?

Him: They're coming with. They call me Uncle Duane Duane.

Does CEO Kiffin deserve it? Maybe. Still, I find myself breaking for him.

Duane Duane (watching me fidget): Don't you fink out on me, Paul.

I nod, run a hand through my hairdo. A clump of Tuscan Umber falls out. I replace it but Duane Duane is already chuckling.

Him: I know your hair is canned, Paul. That's obviously an aerosoled part. Who are you kidding?

I'm flushed and trembling, worried what else he might have figured out. I could use some Dignity-in-a-Can. Or Nothing-in-the-Can-in-a-Can. I try to coolly laugh it off. I try to waddle without looking like I'm waddling. I might split at the seams. I fear there is, and has always been, a blatant comical bulge in the seat of my pants.

Then HR Pete stops in to inquire about a PSU on Pandora's Pogz.

Him (eyeing me with my disheveled canned hair): Paul, please don't take this the wrong way, but you don't look so swell. Maybe you should take a seat and level your breathing?

Duane Duane stares at me.

HR Pete (pointing at a chair): Paul, I'm sorry to give you guff and be such a Debbie Downer, but I'm requesting you please consider possibly sitting and maybe also perhaps placing your head between your knees like the fainting prevention memo suggests?

I wonder if HR Pete is just mocking me, knowing I can't sit.

Me (quick-thinking): I just stood over the heating vent too long is all.

Duane Duane eases his desk drawer shut, gives me a discreet thumbs-up.

HR Pete: I guess I'll suggest maybe filling out a Medical Event Description just in case?

I nod. He leaves for his indoor soccer game and I lean on my desk, maintaining a posture both nonchalant and considerate of the lightbulb.

Duane Duane (winking): Good stuff, Paul! The heating vent was a nice touch.

Then he gives me a firm congratulatory slap on the rear.

And there is a definite and immediate internal shattering.

My gut is suddenly one ornery porcupine. I think of MD Kowalski's puns tomorrow. All kidding aside. I miss Moxy. With the recent frosts, CEO Kiffin must be ice fishing by now. Has he caught that helluva humdinger? I wonder if he'll think it was worth it. That fucking cuckold. I'm thinking his plastic-bottle gin habit is the effect of much more than just a failing career. The only thing more fearful to a man than his own failure is his emotional vulnerability. I made a promise I'm not sure is right to keep. But I still promised. I can only assume Admin Gwynn loops the yo-yo string on her finger before frontally corking it.

Note to self: Maybe attach all future random tailpipe objects to string?

I bite my lip. Duane Duane takes the tackle box.

Him (giving my arm a friendly jab): Sorry we never got that beer.

There is nothing I can say to make this moment more or less pathetic. He puts the tackle box in CEO Kiffin's office. Then the front door shuts. And that is that.

In Production, I keep busy with leaky oil tankers and slick, ebony gull designs, ignoring the occasional sharp pain when I move too suddenly or awkwardly. It's like my guts and lower back are up against a cheese grater. I check my email and find the standard reply from HR Pete thanking me for my great EFFA input. Is it my place to get involved? Does CEO Kiffin even care? Does Mrs. Kiffin, VP want to be saved by her husband? Is she testing him? Do I have any obligation to either man? I feel like the last time I stood in MD Kowalski's office: him staring, me standing and deciding whether to confess my situation or not. A promise is a promise. But I didn't know what I was promising. What is protocol?

Me (cursing myself): *Fink fink fink!*

I waddle into CEO Kiffin's office and remove four pogs from the tackle box. On each blank back I write a letter in thick marker: U - T - A - H. Then I return them. To play, you stack pogs facedown and slam the stack with a metal slammer. You retain the ones that flip face-up. Then you restack the rest and the next person slams. The winner is the person who flips over the most pogs. My stance: if I were CEO Kiffin and cared enough to find my wife, I'd leave no pog unturned. I'd figure it out. I'd win. This is the best I can do.

I waddle to the water cooler and take careful sips. Then I hear a singsong *Yoo-hoo!* Admin Gwynn leans against the Postal cubicle with a yo-yo, nose whistling with each flick of her wrist. She Rocks the Baby, Walks the Moxy.

Admin Gwynn (winking): Care to join me in Postal?

The yo-yo spins down up, down up, down up. I notice the mail bin's shoe scuff marks, the radiator's handcuff scrapes. I shrug.

Her (maybe joking or maybe not): Or would you prefer I put the yo-yo up your tailpipe, if that's the sort of thing you're into?

I'm into that, sure. But I don't want her to, besides the obvious. Why? Is there a right or wrong answer? Why do I care what she thinks? Us both creatures of habit. The way I've chosen to live my life has brought me to this moment, and I wonder by voluntarily withholding myself, not unlike CEO Kiffin, am I like him? Trivial and forgotten?

My eyes well. I shiver, suddenly terrified of dying alone. My pelvis burns.

Admin Gwynn pockets the yo-yo. She surprises me by placing a hand on my shoulder.

Her (concerned): Is something wrong, Paul? You don't look so *hawt.*

She exhibits a depth I didn't know she was capable of. Maybe that means I have depth, too. I appreciate her hand on me, breathless and strange with relief.

Me: I'm taking a sick day tomorrow.

Admin Gwynn: What's wrong?

Me (oddly sincere): I'm currently clandestine.

Admin Gwynn (raising her eyebrows): You poor baby!

She moves her hand to my cheek, and I lean into that lotioned sun and just photosynthesize. I can feel myself between every line of her palm, between her fake red fingernails. Those pretty press-on sympathies holding my head up. It feels good and right. Still, I could split her like a wishbone and noodle her: me, paper-bagged. Still, I could let her stone my heart with her breathy kisses. Still, I could get slammed. Still, I could open myself up and maybe be received truly by her. Still, I could find out the hard way if it's all worth it or not. Still, my quivering WIIFM? eyes. Still, I see my skeletons reflecting in her bowling ball pupils as several strikes thunder below our feet, a near tribute. Still, I could be wronged, unaccepted. Still, I fear more never having the chance. Still, a gamble.

Still, still, still.

Me: Let's maybe just take it slow and get a cup of coffee sometime?

Admin Gwynn blushes.

Her (nose twittering): I knew it! I knew you wouldn't come into the Postal cubicle with me. I know what's in there.

She pokes me in the torso and it takes every ounce of me not to yelp.

Me (gulping and nervous and pin-cushioned): What?

Her (batting wispy-lashed hazel eyes): A gentleman, *duh?*

I shrug, not really knowing.

She locks up Pogz and shyly takes my hand and out we go.

Small fuzzy snowflakes sweep back and forth in symphonies. My cold ears feel like Styrofoam packing peanuts when I rub them. The front of the Bowl-O-Drome is covered with tarps and scaffolding. The sign is broken. Only *Bowl* flickers neon, and I mistake it for *Bowel* and wonder, How many MD Kowalskis does it take to unscrew a busted lightbulb? I strategically wince, waddling beside Admin Gwynn to her car. She offers me a ride but I respectfully decline. I've got to take the bus. I'll stand even with seats available.

Near the bus stop, a municipal worker in an orange vest spray-paints telephone poles, marking where sewer lines will need to be dug up and repaired next year. He sprays an *S*, then an arrow pointing at the sidewalk. From here it looks like the vertical initials *S.I.V.* They've been fixing the sewer lines since the tornado. It's a year for repair. Somewhere a dog goes postal, howling out its vulgar throat. A group of janitors exit the tarps covering the damaged Bowl-O-Drome's entrance, name-patched DOUG and JOSE and IAN. The wind shifts just right and I get a sour whiff of the Utica reservoir west of the orchard.

Admin Gwynn (bashful): So when do you want to get that cup of coffee?

Me (faint): Maybe after the Friday Pep? I've got some healing to do before then.

And what Admin Gwynn does next makes me blubber like a baby once I've clambered onto the bus, hunching in the aisle among empty plastic seats and sitting passengers curiously and uncomfortably eyeing me. Me, blubbering so hard that the replaced clump of Tuscan Umber looses as the bus bounces and my guts curse me out. The windows steam up from the heat of us all, and one passenger distracts herself from me by drawing a heart with her finger on the fogged pane and then pierces it with an arrow. Tomorrow I'll be reduced to a pun. But here, in the parking lot, what feels like my guts digesting barbed wire, I am witnessing a beginning. And I believe Admin Gwynn will receive me at whatever depth I possess. Because what Admin Gwynn does next has never been done to me, and I'm struck with an urgent desire to confide in her. Be my muse, Gwynn. Teach me what is protocol. I want to tell her how sad the corks really make me. How as a kid I was pinched all over by a woman in the ball pit of a McDonald's PlayPlace, and she left bruises. How I once let Moxy lick peanut butter off my lifegiver. How the woman in the PlayPlace knelt and showed me crooked front teeth when she smiled. How she had a forearm tattoo of a shark that disappeared under the colored balls, and there were pinches I could not see and could not explain and could not heal. How I sometimes sit outside the McDonald's PlayPlace and rub my knuckles raw on the curb. Tell me I'll be all right, Gwynn. Be my experiment. I want to acquire something new. So sue me, please. I'm for seriously begging.

What Admin Gwynn does next is she grabs my Dynamo! tie and pulls me close. I can smell her herbal shampoo and minty blemish cream again. Someone is trying to relocate my guts with a pitchfork. I curl my numbing toes. My lifegiver, patient this time. She puts her mouth to the side of my head. Her nose, whistling like a sunrise. Her hot, generous breath like a fever over the pink packing-peanut ear I meet halfway to offer her. Here in the flurried parking lot, tears assembling, preparing to flank me on the bus.

Her (for serious): Let me take care of you.

Acutely Angled

and I miss the tug of the rod, the crank of the reel, the stench of algae, the bob of my dinghy, the piney taste of gin, but I don't miss tangling up tipsy in the fishing net and slipping into the lake's murky blackness, where I swear that two-hundred-pound monster sturgeon swam right by me: bubbles burping, chortling triumphantly as my lungs filled with plankton and my heart quit scratching and ticking like an insect trapped in the kitchen light fixture my wife Selma constantly nagged me to fix, but I thirsted to fill the void in me with two hundred pounds of monster sturgeon proudly arched over my mantle, and I miss the first forty years of my life, the lost second forty, the forty-foot creaky dock warped like the spine of an old woman or old man that I won't become, and I miss the flashes of fireflies at dusk while playing tackle football with my boys, the flashes of leaping salmon at dawn while arranging my tackle box, and I miss painting Selma's toenails, painting my lures, and I miss Selma's slick tanned flesh as she skinny-dipped in our pool late at night, the slick sandy scales of the monster sturgeon taunting me before dipping down into the fluid blackness, and I miss the infrequent intercourse, of course, with Selma: her casting and reeling my bobbing dangler, and I miss Selma's round stomach, where I'd listen to my fetal boys' hearts strongly bate, baiting hooks with slippery night crawlers, and I miss the way my infant sons curled in my hands, the curls of the line cast into the crisp air, and I miss Selma's rare bubbly chortles and the prickly touch of those often unshaven legs I ached to kiss and cry against and leave my legacy in teeth marks sometimes, and I even miss the hideous condemning vein in her taut neck, each vane of my dinghy's purring propeller, and I do miss my wife's beautiful bone structure: that acutely angled skull of hers, the scullers gliding through the morning fog like wooden storks, and I miss the taste of scrambled eggs with fresh salmon, the late night scrambled pornography when Selma made up the couch for me, and I really miss my young boys and their photo refrigerator magnets and every bedtime story I never read but should have, the wind whistling through the shore reeds and my thinning unaccomplished hair, and I miss menthol cigarettes, the silhouette of Selma fluidly gliding past the couch that I should have reached out for and stopped just once when she'd visit my nightmared children and lovingly gather them up under one blanket with her and I'd hear their whispers and her tired bubbly chortles, and I miss being a part of that blackness with them, and I won't miss this chum heart and the endless casting of these threads dangling from my torso like pale soggy kelp until I reach that Great Lake Erie in the Sky, but what I miss most of all is being able to tell Selma and my boys that I'm sorry and they were my everything even if it didn't seem that way, and I wish they could know just how much I love – but wait! here come those slick sandy scales, and oh I got you this time: hook, line, and sinker! and I cast another thread and stick my translucent face under the water and let the plankton fill my liquor-bottle lungs, and I hiccup out a few minnows and this is now my everything: my head is the world's biggest fish tank, and I think I hear the bubbled chortling coming from somewhere in the blackness, and I get the curse words ready in my mouth and then that silhouetted monster just glides right by, and I miss

Tighter, Goodbye

Snapmare is certain the birds are from Ma and Pa.

He'd been in his room, wrestling thoughts about Polly. Will she reciprocate his feelings or reject them? Then these two robins landed on his sill, their beautiful copper breasts speaking to him. They embraced, chirped, flew off to a telephone wire.

So now Snapmare is up, decided. He dresses in Pa's decorated police uniform, his finest attire. Polishes the badge. Leaves the pistol holster empty. Combs his hair to properly conceal the scar serrated across the left side of his head. Examines his dapper image in the mirror. Places Ma's wedding ring in his breast pocket.

Through the duplex dividing wall, Snapmare hears Ingrid's cassette tape player – the high-pitched scrambling as she forwards and rewinds to locate sounds of crying. Always and only, this distinct recorded crying. Along with the cries, he hears television game shows and her gibberish, a product of her cough syrup habit. She guzzles, an antiqued pinky finger mournfully extended. Says prairies to photographs of her dead cats and young grandson.

Not *prairies*, Snapmare thinks, concentrating.

The wreck during the '92 snowstorm left Snapmare aphasic. Words jumble, linger at the tip of his randomly inarticulate tongue. Ma and Pa carpooled to heaven. Life insurance remedied little. Snapmare nine-to-fives at the KwikStop, clerking beside his freckled crush, Polly. He's training to become the professional wrestling tag team partner of his buddy Nimrod. Wants Polly to be his redheaded ringside diva, hear her cheering him on from just outside the ropes. The scar on his head is an intimidating accessory, the difference between one heartbeat and the next. That difference being everything.

Down the hall, Tiff's door is closed. Snapmare guesses she is writing more poetry about the crash, using internal organ metaphors for engine parts beside stick figures with the left arms and legs scribbled out. He wipes his nose with a pinching motion: a nervous habit. Wonders, What did she do with the pink carnations? Peeks through the keyhole, spots a man with green hair and pierced nipples hugging his bathrobed sister vigorously from behind. One arm is tattooed like a python: eyes on the knuckles, a tongue winding along the inside of his thumb. The man makes the hand into a snapping mouth. Hisses, elated.

Tiff's childhood wallpaper is faded in just the right places so the pirouetted ballerinas' faces are blank, indiscriminate. The belt on the carpet has a buckle of two dice rolled snake eyes. The trash can holds the bouquet of carnations. Snapmare frowns at them. Beside the bed Tiff's prosthetic left arm and leg lean like two tangible nightmares.

The floorboards groan under Snapmare. Through the door Tiff explains how Mr. Vegas has commissioned her to help him become an EMT. The new technique is called the Horizontal Heimlich. Requires meticulous practice. They have to be almost nude because it's easier for a novice to find the abdomen without the impediment of fabric.

But she lies.

Just like when Mr. Milwaukee commissioned her to help him become a Marine. Tiff counted push-ups beneath him. Had to be almost nude to properly scrutinize form. Like when Mr. Dallas hired her to help him practice for the rodeo. Tiff simulated the bucking bull. Had to be almost nude because bareback riding is more difficult than saddled. Just like all the others: Mr. Cincinnati, Mr. Toronto,

Mr. Orlando, Mr. Newark, etc. All carrying airport luggage, though none of them ever stayed long enough to need it.

Snapmare rolls his eyes. Who is she trying to fool?

Snapmare pinches his nose and tells Tiff he's running an errand, patting Ma's wedding ring in his pocket. Thinks of the robin's coppery breast, Polly's long coppery hair. Polly is working a shift at the KwikStop. Today is Snapmare's day off. Today is going to change the meaning of everything. He sits at the bus stop and considers Ingrid's *prairies.* Imagines Ingrid kneeling over the photographs of her dead cats and grandson, her spindly fingers intersected, eyes squeezed shut, fuzzy upper lip cough-syruped purple.

Thinks, *Prairies prairies prairies.*

*   *   *

Mr. Vegas concludes the Horizontal Heimlich, dresses.

Out the window, children pick teams for Wiffle ball. The scrawniest kid gets picked last. Tiff tucks bangs behind a flushed ear, waiting for the moment to turn as it always does while the airport men dress. The moment when their endearment ends. The sudden reality of the situation. The moment when the men become ashamed of her and flee.

Fake endearment is still endearment, Tiff justifies. But she lies.

The moment turns. Mr. Vegas lets his tongue pant from his chapped mouth, observing the late afternoon light fingering beneath Tiff's bathrobe, tickling at the beginnings of the alleged *erased* side. Licks his lips. Wants to see her scars. Tugs the bathrobe. Wants to see where the limbs are supposed to go. So punk. Tells her she is beautiful all broken.

Tiff slaps his face, cries out. Mr. Vegas covers her mouth.

Ingrid turns up her tape player, her television: guess the price; win the dinette set; cry.

Mr. Vegas tugs open the bathrobe. Ogles the raised glossy scars, the two partial limbs puckered like suspended kisses. So punk. Throats a purr, shivers.

Tiff kicks at Mr. Vegas and hits the belt buckle. Mr. Vegas groans, hisses through gapped teeth. Raises the python. The tongue tattoo on his palm spirals inward like a bull's-eye. Tiff cringes. The moment becomes brutally honest.

Ingrid's television audience cheers. The announcer hoots.

Mr. Vegas tells Tiff he lied when he said she was beautiful.

Tiff nods. "I know."

*   *   *

Snapmare finds the correct word: Ingrid's *prayers*.

He sighs, relieved. Imagines the Wernicke area of his temporal lobe as a disorganized filing cabinet, a copier with a paper jam, a junkyard. Down the street a game of Wiffle ball commences. Potholes are bases. Home plate is a pile of curbed black trash bags loitering like the Polish mechanics who smoke outside the Bowl-O-Drome. One of the boys has wrapped his Wiffle ball bat with aluminum foliage.

Not *foliage*, Snapmare thinks, concentrating. Pictures aluminum *foliage*'s crumpling sound, its silvery sheen, knows it can't be microwaved. Recalls how he and Polly met while stacking boxes of it on his first day at the KwikStop.

Thinks, *Foliage foliage foliage.*

Polly's unconventional whistling instantly intrigued Snapmare. The peculiar way he combs his hair invited her curiosity. They stacked boxes of aluminum *foliage* and chatted, discovering they'd both attended Upstate CC. Polly studied ornithology. Shared whistled impersonations of loons, owls, mallards. Snapmare dropped out after the accident to train as Nimrod's tag team partner. Shared several maneuvers gently on her until it aroused him. Went back to stacking aluminum *foliage* with a hunched posture.

Foil! Snapmare retrieves. He straightens his tie.

A Wiffle ball swerves up to the telephone line and strikes a robin. The other birds break into beautiful violent trysts above the street, capturing Snapmare's attention. A boy rounds the pothole bases. Nobody notices the struck robin helicoptering to the sidewalk. The other birds reconvene on the line squawking, disgruntled.

After stacking aluminum foil, Snapmare and Polly didn't want to go home. They punched out, went miniature golfing. Polly shuddered when two golfers argued. The divorce is escalating: the accusing, the cheating, the broken kitchenware. Polly is another chipped saucer. She eats with paper plates and plastic utensils. After a fight Polly's father hugs her, which means he's leaving for a while. The tighter the hug, the longer the goodbye. The hugs are getting tighter. Ornithology fascinates Polly because of the aerial freedom, the ease of escape. She has a pet parakeet named Keet that she confides in. Asked Snapmare, Did he know hummingbirds could fly backward? That the pitohui has poisonous feathers? That storks have no call because they lack a syrinx? Snapmare didn't, but logged all the facts on paper in his wallet. Polly told him her parents took little interest in the facts. Nobody ever did.

Snapmare explained the peculiar way he combs his hair: to cover the scar, his malfunctioning Wernicke area. He described the weightlessness of a vehicle spinning over ice. The headlights screaming into the driver's-side windows, fragmenting through the frost into one thousand slivers. The collision. Pieces of glass brushed Snapmare's face like childhood bedtime stories. Seat belts hugged tighter, goodbye. Each heartbeat a lifetime. Between heartbeats lingered a memory of a Fourth of July: he and Tiff throwing a Frisbee. How Tiff was silhouetted in the bruising evening just before the fireworks exploded. How she trailed the Frisbee, anticipating the give-and-take of the breeze. How ably she laughed and ran.

Polly touched his hand then. Snapmare allowed the good memory to linger.

Polly has softly tiptoed her teacup heart and on numerous occasions attempted to investigate it, only to be quickly reminded of the sharp specific sounds of specific dishes shattering between her parents in the kitchen.

The bus pulls up. Snapmare boards.

Through each intersection, he almost feels the turbulent weightlessness again. Squeezes the armrests. An unpleasant odor revolves around the mustached driver. An elderly woman with bunched stockings fiddles with a hearing aid. The ads are Sharpied with lewd graffiti. The graspable leather loops for standing passengers sway like impatient nooses. The potholes, Wiffle ball bases, give the bus natural percussion: *thump thump thump.*

Snapmare takes the paper from his wallet:

Storks have no call because they lack a syrinx.

Penguins, ostriches & dodos can't fly.

A duck's quack doesn't echo.

The bus stops. People get off. People get on.

Snapmare feels a tap on his shoulder. Nimrod sits, wearing his camouflage spandex costume. His lopsided pecs twitch. Abs like truck pistons. A helmet supporting buck antlers from Uncle Angelo's Taxidermy Villa casts shadows like winter tree limbs.

Professional wrestling personas fascinate Snapmare. Life inside the ring is organized. Life outside the ring seems so only in retrospect, after it has complicated further. The persona allows for victory, in the ring, in the head, in the heart.

Snapmare has only wrestled once, a local tournament. Nimrod paid the entry fee, a birthday gift. In the ring everything slowed, simplified. Snapmare's mind shifted up into another gear. A white-hot instinct, like piercing high beams. He became muscle-memoried. Nearly broke his opponent's arm. The bell rang several times before Snapmare heard it, downshifting. Released his squealing opponent. Snapmare wiped his enormous wet forehead. Nimrod slapped his back, grinning. Told him he was born to brawl.

"You brawl today?" Snapmare asks, tucking the facts into his breast pocket.

"No, bub. Soon, I hope. Them tryouts is in eight weeks. Healthy this go. Just got these made. Gives me an edge." Nimrod opens an envelope and exhibits photos of himself dressed as his persona: The Mighty Nimrod. He stands in front of a curtain painted like a forest, bending a rubber rifle, lifting a plastic log over his head, uppercutting a taxidermied bear.

Snapmare points to the uppercut, "What's that?"

"Them's a difficult maneuver, bub. For professionals only. Learned it from watching reruns of old Punchy Phillips fights on cable."

"But I got to know it if I'm going to be your pardoner," he replies. "I mean *partner*."

Nimrod tucks the photos away. "I told you, bub. You can't be my partner. I'm ruttin' for heavyweight champ. Them tag teamers is just a sideshow act."

Snapmare has always known this. But he considers the alternative: outside the ring. Wipes his nose with a pinching motion.

The bus stops. People get off. People get on.

Nimrod readjusts his antlers, grins. "Tiff get them pink carnations?"

Snapmare recalls the pink carnations in his sister's trash can. The prosthetic limbs just beyond them like squandered vases. Nimrod signed every card *Secret Admirer*. Every item he sent to Tiff she immediately discarded.

Snapmare gulps, nods.

"And?"

"And she liked them?" Snapmare says.

Nimrod glows. "I knew we was destined right off when she didn't look askance at them antlers! Just inquisitively, and rightfully so." An antler gets stuck in a leather loop. A hair-in-a-canned businessman stands in the aisle, looking askance. Notices Snapmare in the decorated police uniform, nods respectfully. Nimrod pops the antler free of the leather loop, banging his elbow, rubbing the fresh lump that rises. "I remember Tiff said a carnation is simultaneously beautiful and violent like a scrum of doves. Them florist only had pink."

"Pink is her favorite?" Snapmare offers.

Nimrod puffs his chest, "See! My guts told me pink was good! Got to trust the guts! Them'll mean more to her. Them's how you get the girl, bub. Them seemingly unimportant details everybody else overlooks? You make a big humungous deal."

Snapmare tries to recall a detail about Polly he might have overlooked.

"She mention the card? Dotted the *i* in *Secret Admirer* with a heart this time."

"Made her salami?" Snapmare concentrates. "I mean *smile.*"

The bus stops. Nimrod hoots. "I'll tell you what, bub. The only thing I can think of worse than this," he says, demonstrating the uppercut, "is bein' damn lonesome. My luck's sure lookin' up!" Snapmare agrees, patting Ma's ring in his pocket. Nimrod steps off the bus. The antlers clatter. Passengers gossip. The bus driver hems and haws.

From the sidewalk Nimrod turns. "But I wish I could see them smile myself."

Snapmare nods, agrees.

The doors shut on an antler. Nimrod yanks it free just as the bus moves.

*   *   *

147

The python lunges, slithering so punk over Tiff's residual limbs where the scars come together like red fireworks in static explosion. Tiff acknowledges her phantom limbs. Scratches at imaginary itches, wiggles invisible toes and fingers. A red handprint unfolds across her face. Her lower lip swells romantically. She concentrates on her heartbeat. Worries what other parts of her might be phantom, too.

The python licks an armpit scar. Mr. Vegas throats a purr. Tiff focuses her attention on the pink carnations in the trash. Maybe the Secret Admirer is the retired judge with the sick wife: Mr. LA? The Indian podiatrist: Mr. Austin? The department store Santa: Mr. NY, NY? She ponders their fake endearment. Understands that as the moment turns, so does the meaning of everything, so do promises. Promises can't be permanent truth, only temporary. A promise is only meant in its isolated moment. A promise is just an eventual lie.

Like someone who promises to love you forever will break your heart.

Like someone who promises to be there forever will leave you.

But the airport men are the exception, Tiff thinks. Moments turn but they're still meaningless, still liars. No expectations with them, no disappointment. To avoid promises, love a liar. Never let a promise be made, never let it go unfulfilled.

Still, as the python kisses a thigh scar, Tiff finds herself hoping one liar will come along and save her. The fairy-tale prince of her youth. Make her believe in his promises. Make her believe in that impossible Happily Ever After.

Mr. Vegas pinches a hip scar. So punk. Purrs.

A nearby mirror reflects Tiff's glossy red fireworks. She is reminded of a Fourth of July, throwing a Frisbee with her brother. How without hesitation he released the Frisbee to her. How she chased and believed in that offering from him, anticipating the breeze, leaping without question for it. She misses those days, her brother. Blames her shut door. Shut for good reason. Mr. Vegas slithers over a belly laceration. She doesn't want her brother to see her this way. Wants to be recalled as the girl on that summer occasion. She recalls not watching the fireworks collectively. Rather, she chose one individual ember as it escaped the furious center and followed it until it fizzled out and vanished alone into the night. She remembers fearing what happened to the fizzled embers once they faded away. Remembers the moment becoming terrifying. Remembers doing this over and over again.

*   *   *

Nimrod flexes in the mirror. Slips on a blazer over his costume. Pins a pink carnation to it, pricks a finger. A tear of blood blooms. He hopes Tiff will put two and two together and smile. He hopes to see that smile for himself.

He walks to her home. A flagpole outside the duplex has a police precinct flag fluttering at half-mast. Nimrod salutes it, hand to antlers. In a game of street Wiffle ball the scrawniest kid strikes out swinging. The pitcher says, "*Cha-ching!*" Robins heckle from the telephone wire. Another limps on the sidewalk below, twittering softly.

Nimrod rings the doorbell. Nobody answers. Curtains flap in an open window. Nimrod peeks in. A green-haired man with an arm tattooed like a snake rubs himself all over Tiff. He sees Tiff's scars, like asterisks. The puffy handprint on her cheek waves hello.

His heart rallies. Muscles territorially bulge. He snorts, clambers inside.

The antlers clatter. Tiff catches his reflection in the far wall mirror. She gasps, clutches her bathrobe shut. The green-haired man jumps up, shrieks. Nimrod throws an uppercut and topples him. Body-slams him as if soaring from the top turnbuckle.

The volume of Ingrid's television increases: spin the wheel; go bankrupt.

The man's eyes water, mascara streaks. Nimrod sits on his back and bends his legs into a figure-four cloverleaf hold. Tucks a leg under his armpit and yanks. The man makes a noise that resembles air escaping the pinched mouth of a balloon.

Ingrid's television amplifies: buy a vowel; solve the puzzle.

The python slaps the carpet in agony.

Responding instinctively to a tap out, Nimrod releases. The man scrambles out the window. The Wiffle ball game suspends. Children watch the man limp down the street, giggling at his dark denim piss stain. Then the game resumes.

Nimrod wipes his brow, catches his breath, proud of the perfectly executed maneuvers. Hasn't lost a step since his injuries, his setbacks. He's confident about the upcoming tryouts. Tiff trembles against her headboard, clutching the prosthetic limbs like a defense. Nimrod raises his hands, takes a step backward. "Just seen them bub hurtin' you is all. My guts told me you needed help. Brawlin's kind of in my blood like that," he says.

"He wasn't hurting me," Tiff says. She lowers her eyes.

Nimrod gulps. "Them bub ain't your bubfriend is he?"

"I don't have a boyfriend," Tiff says, adjusting a bra strap. "I've met you. You're my brother's friend with the horns."

"Yes. And them is antlers." Nimrod points to his helmet.

Tiff lowers her prosthetics. "Could you?" she asks, making a circle with a finger. "Oh," Nimrod says, nodding. Shuts his eyes, turns around. Hears some fumbling, straps tightening. "I rung them doorbell," Nimrod adds.

"I heard it," Tiff says. "Okay."

Nimrod turns. Tiff looks different with the prosthetics. Like herself before the crash. Thinks she is more herself now without them, more knowledgeable about the other side of the world: its cruel, below-the-belt nature. He knew about bad luck: the pulled groin before the tryouts last year, the broken wrist before that. He hasn't auditioned in years. Has plenty of his own scars. They could trade them. The prosthetics are just plastic lies.

"Please don't stare."

"I didn't mean nothin' by it, honest."

"My brother isn't home."

Nimrod blushes. "Them ain't why I'm here."

Tiff scrunches her face, confused. Nimrod puffs his chest, emphasizes his blazer. Tiff notices the pinned pink carnation. She puts two and two together. Nimrod blushes harder. He takes another step backward.

But Tiff doesn't smile. Her eyes widen. Looks to Nimrod's feet.

Nimrod steps backward, knocks over the trash can. The pink carnations spill out.

The moment becomes silent.

"I guess you're going to leave so you might as well do it," Tiff says.

Nimrod glances to the window.

Tiff waits for the moment to fulfill its turn.

"I'll go when you ask me to," Nimrod says. He picks up the unopened envelope from the flowers and flicks it to her. Tiff anticipates the breeze from the window, catches it. The scrawniest kid hits into a double play. Next door, Ingrid's television goes to a commercial break. A taped cry bawls. The robin in the lawn falls over. Its wing sort of waves in a gust.

Tiff opens the envelope, reads.

"How did you know I think a carnation looks like a scrum of doves?"

"I remembered from the poem you read in your Ma and Pa's eulogy."

"You dotted the *i* with a heart." Tiff touches her mouth. Nimrod twiddles his thumbs. He observes the handprint on her cheek. Desires to kiss it, heal it.

"I should get some ice for them swellin'," he says.

"Wait," Tiff says, grabbing Nimrod's hand. "Just stay with me a minute?"

"Okay." He sits beside her. Tiff rereads the card, squeezes Nimrod's hand. Nimrod gently squeezes back, reassuring her he is still right there.

*   *   *

The KwikStop Muzak plays behind the buzz of a dilapidated ice cream chest leaking a small puddle of cream. The colorful window advertisements filter the incoming light so the various conveniences look as if they are made of stained glass. Bernie is the other clerk on duty, wearing padlocks for earrings, snorting lines of Pixy Stix off a comic book. Snapmare asks for Polly. Bernie inhales, rolling his eyes, tickled by the sugar buzz. Tugs a depressed earlobe, nods toward the back. "Cig break," he grunts.

But Polly doesn't smoke, Snapmare thinks.

The parking lot out back contains two cars and a dumpster perched with strays. Wrappers swirl over the damp pavement, mock derelict autumn. Polly sits on a bumper, her long red hair and smock strings curling flirtatiously in the gusts. Her hands cover her face, her torso hiccups. Bony elbows jut like stubby, flightless chick wings.

Two tabbies spit, leap into the dumpster. She lowers her hands.

Polly's thick glasses magnify tearful eyes.

Snapmare thinks, *Hornbills have long black curling eyelashes.*

Polly's sobs treble and tweet.

Snapmare thinks, *Storks have no call because they lack a syrinx.*

Polly hugs Snapmare. "Keet escaped," she says. She was petting him while her parents fought. Keet nibbled peanut shells. Polly confided. How could her parents argue like this? Could they have ever loved each other? Was it a lie from the beginning?

Then another dish shattered in the kitchen: Gram's hand-painted ceramic platter.

Startled, Keet flew from Polly's finger out a window.

Each of her sobs dizzies Snapmare. Like he was spinning in the weightless vehicle again. Like when he and Polly were in a matinee at the Cineplex and her parents called, lobbying her to choose a side, a person to live with. An onscreen concession stand ad pictured two cartoon candy bars eating each other. Like when he was recently with Polly at the Bowl-O-Drome when her father showed up and told her they were definitely going to part, giving Polly his wedding band and her mother's ring. Hugged her tighter than he ever had. A nearby 7–10 split teetered at the calamity of her father's indifferent use of "*part.*"

"There, there," Snapmare soothes. Polly calms.

"I thought today was your day off," she says, taking in the decorated police uniform, the shiny badge. Polly cocks her head.

Then Snapmare drops to a knee.

"I have generous infection for you," he says.

Not *infection*, he thinks, furrowing. "I mean generous affliction." Snapmare straightens his tie. Imagines the Wernicke area of his temporal lobe as a gummed-up piston, a buzzing ice cream chest leaking cream, a thrift store sofa with a spring bursting through its cushion. The correct word on the very tip of his tongue. Pictures pink carnations, a game of Frisbee, two coppery-breasted robins embracing, a ring.

He reaches into his pocket.

"I have generous erections for you," he says.

Polly blushes, grabs Snapmare's wrist before it leaves his pocket.

Snapmare scrunches, concentrates. Thinks, *Erections erections erections.*

"Don't," she says. "I know. Please, don't say it."

A stray cat rubs against Snapmare's leg. "Why?" he asks.

"Because."

"Because what?"

"Because of what it could mean. What it could become."

"It means what it means," Snapmare says.

Polly shakes her head. "How can you be so sure? Just look at my home!"

Snapmare turns Ma's wedding ring in his pocket. The paper sticks to his sweaty palm. Two bird facts bleed together. He looks at Polly's hands: her father's band on one, her mother's ring on the other. Polly tucks them into her smock.

"A home can be me and you," Snapmare says.

"A home was also once my parents."

"Mine too."

"And Tiff?"

Snapmare recalls the Fourth of July, the Frisbee. Wipes his nose with a pinching motion.

Polly takes a deep breath. "How are we any different? How do we not become that?"

Snapmare thinks but doesn't know. He imagines Tiff with the airport men, the faded wallpaper ballerinas. How can he promise Polly anything about a home with his sister like this? How can she believe him? Pets the tabby. Removes his empty hand from his pocket, stands. A gust pushes Polly's hair up into a brilliant copper flame.

"We are different. We won't become that," Snapmare urges. He holds her tight to rebut that a hug doesn't always mean goodbye, tighter to reassure her there isn't a longer ensuing goodbye, tighter to show her he isn't going anywhere.

But Snapmare knows he needs to do more than just make a promise. Promises are too easy to make. This is why trust is so fragile. He shuffles back into the KwikStop. Polly stands there, allowing the hug to linger.

She fiddles with her parents' rings. Tears flock down her freckled cheeks. The tabby rubs against her leg. She shoos it away and notices a piece of paper blowing across the parking lot. Snatches it before it sucks into a gutter. Unfolds it. Reads the overlooked details. Two have bled together. Finds herself beginning to trust in them:

Hornbills have long black curling eyelashes.
There are more chickens in the world than people.
The kiwi bird of New Zealand has no tail or wings.

* * *

The Wiffle ball game is in the seventh inning stretch. Children hold their caps over their hearts, sing, "Take Me Out to the Ball Game."

The wind picks up, the sky grays. The injured robin squawks in the grass.

Nimrod and Tiff observe the ballerinas on the wallpaper.

"What are we supposed to do?" Tiff says. Nimrod thinks.

"The worst thing anyone can do is be damn lonesome. So them is what we don't do." Tiff rereads the card. Maybe promises can still be the truth. Maybe as meanings change and complicate, the truth only becomes harder to see. Her heart jetés.

She gently squeezes Nimrod's hand.

Nimrod gently squeezes back, heart glittering like the champs belt held above his head.

Tiff touches her bruised cheek, winces.

"I should get some ice to ease them swellin'," Nimrod says.

Tiff believes before he clatters through the door he'll turn back to her. At the door, Nimrod turns, sees the smile he came for. Just as perfect as he imagined.

While Nimrod is gone, Tiff opens her notebook, begins to search for the truths buried somewhere in the new meaning of everything.

* * *

Mr. Vegas dries the piss stain in the airport bathroom. Not so punk. Rubs his sore legs and jaw. Respikes his green hair. Wipes off the mascara on his cheeks, like out-of-tune guitar strings. Avoids his own reflection, the python tattoo. It feels like that tattoo all over. Stuffs that feeling down. Tells himself what happened here will stay here.

But he lies.

The ticket agent confirms his flight. Mr. Vegas focuses on home: the illuminated Strip covered with cabs, hookers, lobster buffets, the adult video rental hut where he alphabetizes. Thinks of his mother asking, How was the trip to his father's? How was the concert? Was it so punk? Is his father seeing anyone? Is she prettier than her? Does this slut make him blueberry pancakes, so fave? Did his father slip up and say he misses her at all?

Mr. Vegas considers the cost of love, curses his niggard heart.

The ticket agent asks if he has any luggage to check.

Mr. Vegas feels his guts coil. He blushes, shakes his head.

* * *

The bus stops. People get off. People get on.

Snapmare finds the correct word: his generous *affection*. He sighs, unrelieved. Considers Fourth of July. Perfect. The last good memory when things seemed so simple before they got complicated.

Life inside the ring could never feel like that. But things would also never be that way again. The fireworks have fizzled. The persona is a lie.

Life outside the ring may be cruel but it's true. What exists inside the ring is an impossible definition of life, of himself. When the match bell rings and he steps outside the ropes, what is it he is afraid to grapple? Everything, he admits. Especially the terror. Snapmare's connection with Tiff has frayed. If he intends to promise Polly he can keep a home, Snapmare knows he needs to promise Tiff first. Prove he is capable. Snapmare needs to be what Tiff has needed all along, what the airport men are for: to be a mutual sufferer, bereaver, carry his share of their experience, their terror. He needs to be the one who catches the Frisbee this time. The one who leaps, without question, for her.

This is life: one the crier, the other the shoulder, Snapmare thinks.

This is life: this constant back-and-forth.

The sky darkens. Rumbles threaten the distance. The wind cools. Robins hop over the grass trying to seduce out the furtive night crawlers preparing to surface in the cool moonlight. What can be seen of the milky moon is low and lucent, nearly full, like a cataractous eye. A child hits a leadoff home run. The injured robin lies quietly near some landscaping. Its companion flutters down and nudges it. The child rounds the pothole bases, celebrates with a Kurt Gibsoned fist pump. Ingrid's game show audience cheers in almost perfect unison.

Snapmare looks into Tiff's window from the sidewalk. She sits hunched, writing. She looks like Ma. Misses her terribly. Snapmare wipes his nose with a pinching motion. He looks closer, notices the handprint, the bruises like criminal fingerprints.

The moment becomes alarmed, punitive, dusk.

Snapmare recalls the screech of rubber tires. His mind shifts up a gear.

Inside, Ingrid's television screeches the telephonic hum of an Emergency Alert System. The taped cries drown out. Mr. Vegas's luggage is in the foyer. None of the men ever stay this long. Snapmare looks down the hall to Tiff's shut door. Fists clench ghost white.

From Pa's closet he retrieves the pistol. In the cold light Snapmare notices his reflection. He looks like Pa. Misses him terribly. Hopes Pa would be proud of him. Thinks that though life is complicated now, it is actually simple compared to the future, where it will only complicate more. This truth calms Snapmare, steadies his hand. Hopes he has what it takes to promise this, believes he does. This is my home, he thinks. Fills the pistol holster.

The floorboards groan outside Tiff's door. Snapmare tightens his tie, straightens the badge. Thinks Mr. Vegas will be taught a lesion.

Not *lesion*, he thinks, concentrating. Thinks of his Wernicke area as a waterlogged pistol, a bullet with a bad primer.

Thinks, *Lesion lesion lesion.*

Doesn't wipe his nose with a pinching motion. Kicks open the door.

The moment turns.

*   *   *

Just before the moment turns. Just before an aproned wife spots the robin lying still in her lawn and calls for her husband to get a shovel. Just before what the wife mistakes for a car backfiring. Just before what Ingrid thinks is thunder and closes her window. Just before the thunder and lightning and rain and coins of hail, the clouds going blacker, swirling and funneling. Just before Ingrid shuts off her television, removes her teeth, swigs the last of the grape cough syrup and whispers a final prayer to the cats and grandson. Just before all of this, the Wiffle ball game concludes. The scrawniest kid delivers the winning RBI. The children hurrah, carry him off. The pitcher kicks loose gravel. The street clears.

Nimrod presses a frozen sirloin to Tiff's face. Tiff leans into him, feels a fresh bruise of his own, a lump on his elbow. Nimrod holds strong, shy to wince. Tiff touches an antler lovingly, pulls him closer, the tightest yet.

The floorboards groan outside her door. Tiff knows it's her brother. Wishes he could see her there with Nimrod, relishing each moment, beside the man who rescued her. She decides to leave the door open from now on. She wants to see her brother. Maybe with a little luck, her brother won't speak through it either and just come right in this time.

And he will.

But just before Snapmare comes right in. Just before Nimrod gives Tiff a soft kiss to the handprint on her cheek. Just before Tiff puts her hand to his lopsided chest to feel for his heartbeat, trust in it. Just before all of this, Nimrod points out the window. Tiff follows. A young woman stands in the lawn. The strengthening gusts lift her curling smock strings, push her hair up into a large teardrop of fire. Thick glasses enlarge her patient eyes. With relentless certainty, she leans into each violent gust, hands clasped in front of her. Looking closer, Tiff notices her hands cup something. Whatever she holds the wind might take it. Something she doesn't want to lose. There, tighter in her hands, the meaning of everything. Something she's afraid might escape. But she holds strong, refusing to let it fly away.

The Cry

"Did you hear him?" the old lady asked. She eased from her golf cart and clutched Emily's waist. Mid-hug, Emily wondered with strange trepidation if maybe this additional weight resembled being with child. A huge button on the lady's shawl tapped against Emily's vacant belly like a knock-knock joke. Who's there? she imagined.

The woman's shawl was covered in cat hair. Emily shuddered, though she admired cats: their nine lives and landing feet first. The problem was the idea of hair – *a tuft of blond hair draping over the star-board gunwale* – Emily's own clumped in the bath drain caused bouts of hyperventilation. She felt the beginnings of another panic attack, eyeing the shawl, and turned her attention to the lady's golf cart: the turn signals, the head- and taillights, a handicap tag on the rearview mirror; in the back, a cardboard box and golf bag toting a cane with a tennis ball knobbed on its end. Emily offered the cane. The lady took it, standing right-angled so each breath dispersed the flour on Emily's apron into a white cloud.

Emily had worked at StickyBunz Bakery in the mall food court since her freshman year at Upstate CC (taking just one hiatus her sophomore year – *The AEΦ sorority boat anchored beneath the sixty-foot-high lake palisades: relaxing on the stern seat with a magazine, condensating water bottle between her legs, tanning lotion, a greasy film on her sun-prickled skin, a faint cawing? a single crow laughing? echoing off the palisades' rock face, high-pitched, amplifying, cawing right above her, still a bird? no, a ball of pink in blue shorts, clipping starboard, the dense thud, the boat violently jostling, bucked to starboard, big splash, cold lake water speckling her face, rippling, bubbles, some red on the lake surface, a tuft of blond hair draping over the starboard gunwale –*). She progressed from free sample distributor to manager.

Today after work, Costaki, Upstate Gardens' handsome door-man, mentioned that the golf cart lady had asked for Emily. But he refused to let her in. He didn't recognize her. Emily uncertainly didn't either – *the old woman weeping over the short empty casket, standing beside a chinless Lake Patrol officer at a lectern, announcing no signs of foul play, but where was the boy? where had his body gone?* – Costaki had rubbed his tan nape, observing the grout grids of the floor tiles. Emily blushed, twirling her bangs.

"He's gone! *Gone!*" the woman said.

The old woman wore a purple mustache stain. Her lips wrenched into a lopsided grin, a Picasso muse. Her swollen calves, bruised yellow like state fair squash. A shunt hung from her neck like a baby pacifier. She rummaged through her purse, wheezing.

A paperback fell to the grass as the lady pulled out a half-empty grape cough syrup bottle. Emily picked up the book and read the title: *The Nuance of the Cry* by Dietrich P. Loewe, MD. Curious, she flipped to the contents:

I. Introduction: The Theory behind *The Nuance of the Cry*
   a. Physiology of Tears in Paradigmatic Relation
   b. Vocalization versus Mute Interiority
   c. Inflection, Expression, and Other
      Verbal Archetypal Stressors
   d. Specific Oral Intonations as Aurally Identifiable
II. Loewe's Eleven Types of the Cry
   The Environmental Cry
   The Desire Cry
   The Sad Cry

After the lady took a swig, Emily returned the book. It was spring. Winter was an afterthought. Earlier, the bus stop bench had kissed Emily's pants, leaving a hyphen of dirt and road salt. Remaining snow melted and pooled into old news.

"Or maybe you saw him?" the lady asked, wiping her purple mouth.

Maybe the woman lost one of her cats? Emily remembers the story about the tornado eight months ago when a girl's parakeet escaped. During the wind and hail and lightning, it returned, as if dropped out of the sky, back through the window, unharmed.

"Did you lose your cat?" Emily asked, peeking under a shrub.

The lady shook her head. "I'm Ingrid Soboloski. My grandson fell into your boat."

– waking from night terrors, sitting upright in a cold sweat, like lake water speckling her face, mother humming lullabies after each horrible dream, whispering "Darling Little Sugar Plum, Emmy," like years and years before in her pigtailed childhood –

The caps of Emily's ears reddened and burned as when they'd been pierced as a girl. What she'd placed on her mind's back burner began to move forward. Snapshots flashed: blue shorts, an insurance claim form with the phrases *cracked starboard gunwale* and *tuft of blond hair.* A blondish ruddy pelt. The entire apartment building of Upstate Gardens suddenly loomed, like the sixty-foot-high lake palisades, The Spot atop them in the trees, where undergrads and local adolescents partied and cliff-jumped. The fire escapes on each stone-façaded side looked like braced buckteeth. Near hyperventilation, Emily felt the need to retreat out of the building's stifling large parallelogramed shadow – *the palisades' large parallelogram shadow, temporary relief from the sun, the shadow lying beyond the buoys where boats are not supposed to be, but a threatening prickle to her dermis, the sensation of sunburning –*

"Let's talk inside," Emily said, helping the old woman by the elbow.

*   *   *

A small shape had been discovered out in the Atlantic, netted by a fishing vessel among a cluster of gasping mackerels. The captain made the sign of the cross. A greenhorn noticed the tiny bloat of its fingers and toes and gagged over port, losing his hat in a gust. The shape was taken inland, unidentified, cremated, and buried in a cemetery beneath a flat blank stone. The shape was a ball: smooth white legs tucked under a jaw, arms hugging hairless shins that jutted from frayed blue swim shorts. One spongy fist clutched a button from a television remote. The button: RECALL. The back was blistered with sunburn that funneled up the nape and branched out to pruned ears like two roses. Muscles tugged the mouth into a grimace, a rigor-mortised jubilation that exposed rusty wire-braced buckteeth: one chipped, hypotenused. The eyelids shut and lashless. The scalp was gone. Only a cranium with what a coroner distinguished as cerebellum matured to approximately seven or so years of age.

*   *   *

"My apologies if this is bad timing," Ingrid wheezed, "but timing is actually why I'm here." She patted her bluish curls, and in the florescent lobby light Emily mapped the horizon of her skull, the constellations of liver spots.

Costaki was signing for packages at his desk. Maybe one was hers, Emily hoped. The contour of his uniform was like a silver lining, one she wouldn't indulge. Not because he might be a disappointment, her hopes for him maybe too high. But because he could be as wonderful as she imagined – and what if *she* was the disappointment to him? She'd spent her whole life dating underachievers because of this feeling of unspectacularness. Still, she adored Costaki's patchy beard that covered acne scars. His naiveté wept down his face in glossy sheets. Sometimes she envisioned little bearded Costakis in diapers, though thoughts of motherhood also instigated near-hyperventilated fits – *the unpredictability and fragility of children, babysitting, sweating, ensuring the baby couldn't – but still worrying it would – find a way to fall from its crib and crack its head open –* So she settled for ordering infomercial junk, elevatoring down to collect the packages and engaging in brief chats.

Costaki looked up, shrugged. Emily smirked, toying with her apron.

Ingrid noticed. She coyly fingered the shunt. "You going with him?"

"What?" Emily blurted. She glimpsed Costaki. Had he heard? He hadn't.

Her last date had been through Kiss&Tell.com. She and the man ate a pleasant dinner, drank too much wine. Afterward they detoured to the Midnite Majestic Motel, drank more boxed wine while decorating a paper bag, which he wore. The bag crinkled as he dropped trou and bared bony thighs and tight briefs, asking what her protocol was on placing a shampoo bottle up someone else's butt? Emily pretended to receive an urgent phone call and taxied home.

Her sixth-floor apartment was still vacant of longed sounds and objects: pattering little feet, husbandly snores, plastic toys littering the carpet, dark stubble festooning the sink. All she collected was laundry for one, sorted in neat hallway piles, the lights and darks and delicates of her life, stains of where she'd been and what she'd done by her lonesome, and as that laundry tumbled and spun, her reflection rippling in the washer/dryer portholes, she couldn't help but stare back at herself and cringe, thinking: *Spinster! Spinster! Spinster!*

"Got to be careful who you go with these days," Ingrid said. "My son, rest his pickled soul, hit Ping-Pong balls at my grandson. Called the welts a bad case of chicken pox. Even chased him with a knife once, accusing him of hiding the television remote. Know where it was? In the man's own shirt pocket! Bless that mailman who intervened. I got custody then. My son liked to pull a cork. History of it in the family. My daughter-in-law had depression. History of that in hers. Their going together brought out the worst in them. My son died a year after my grandson did. Drowned drunk in his tomato soup."

– bubbles in the red dissipating over the lake, white-knuckling the gunwale, frat boys seeing the boy fall from their canoe, paddling as fast as they could back to the dock for help, a good mile away, Lake Patrol eventually offering a shouldered blanket, scuba divers pencil-diving from boats stenciled RESCUE, *red siren lights on the lake, more bubbles –*

Emily blinked.

"But how does a *child* come to terms with ending his life?" Ingrid asked.

They sat on a stiff green and white couch *– the green and white bench seat of the AEΦ boat –* Emily itched, déjà-vued.

"I need to know why he did it. What I did wrong. Why I couldn't help him."

A noise echoed inside Emily, knock-knocking. Who's there? she thought.

"And I need you to help me."

The lady's odd grin hung from her face like a hangnail.

"How?" Emily asked.

"Is it true what you said in the paper? Did you hear him fall?"

– cawing, blue shorts, all that pink skin, what if the boat had been a foot in the other direction? if only tanning had been done on the dock! –

Emily trembled. Some noise olley-olley-oxen-freed inside her. It sounded like a caw. A bird? A single crow laughing? When had she been in the paper? Emily cleared her throat, "Miss Soboloski, is there a chance you might have me confused with someone else?"

Ingrid's mouth twitched. "Emily Jones, Upstate CC and Alpha Epsilon Phi alumnae?"

– Upstate CC's Sorority Row along the lake, the steep zigzagging staircase knifed into the sharp slope leading down to the dock behind Alpha Epsilon Phi, tanning or boating or flashing Chi Phi boys as they canoed by, all that pink skin –

"Yes, but there are lots of Emily Joneses. And Alpha Epsilon Phi is a big sorority."

Ingrid stared back. Her matted pupils waxed and waned as if weighing Emily against the lot of altruisms and atrocities and apologies she'd collected over a lifetime. Emily wondered where she fit into them and for what purpose.

"I suppose there is a chance I'm mistaken. So let's find out." The old woman reached into her purse. "You know, memories aren't forgotten. They just get misplaced sometimes." She hefted out a cassette player and pressed PLAY. A muffled cacophony began: a child's squeaky hiccupping sobs that eventually crescendoed, erupting into terrible gasping wails that stuttered over the phrase *But he said! But he said! But he said!*

Emily was surprised by her own goose bumps and accelerated breaths. Ingrid ejected the tape and held it up. Over a faded date and therapy session number, the word STRESS-INDUCED was scribbled in fresh ink. "I'm sorry you were involved in this," Ingrid said, "and

I'm sorrier to bring it all back. Sorrier yet that my grandson did what he did. Sorrier more for my sorry son. Sorriest that I couldn't help. Maybe I could have. I don't know. And now I am going to die, sooner than later, and I need to know just how sorry I should be. The older you get, the more sorry you feel. You begin to learn just how sorry everything is."

Ingrid paused to sip cough syrup. "I need you to tell me what kind of cry you heard."

Emily craved a cigarette. But smoking wasn't allowed in the lobby. Through the window she saw the golf cart in the lengthening apartment shadow. The cawing inside her felt like a violation, yet honest. She'd taken Anatomy 101 – *the elasticity of joints and ligaments, the largest organ (all that pink skin), bone density and its terrible percussion, the weight of the brain and how it could be damaged psychologically or organically and (combined with Physics 101) if a body, like a car, were cast airborne, the entire vehicle/vessel would begin to tilt as it fell and inevitably land, unlike a cat, engine/head first* – She understood how the mind could lie and trick itself but the body couldn't. Her rapid pulse and aching gut, some ancient dread.

Ingrid placed a frail hand, like a newborn colt, on Emily's clasped and shaking pair. "Please," she whispered, "timing is all I have left and the only thing I don't." This close, Emily noticed that the woman's cheek muscles were stiff from stroke. Her wheeze, grape and ammoniac. Ingrid noticed the hyphen of dirty road salt on Emily's pants, opened her purple mouth, licked a thumb, then pressed it to Emily's thigh, wiping the hyphen away.

"There," Ingrid said, pleased.

"I'm sorry, but I don't know how to help you," Emily said.

Ingrid coughed. "Well," she said, "that is at least a start."

*   *   *

Before being netted, the sunburning balled-up shape was a perch for transatlantic birds to preen, beaks tucked under wings. Gulls discovered the shape in the Atlantic after it spurted from the Hudson River, sucked out by the tide. Along the Hudson's riverbed it had wedged itself into a discarded tire, like a hula-hoop, and remained submerged until the tire was reeled off by a bum on a harbor pier. Upstate Lake channeled into the Mohawk River, a tributary that converged with the Hudson. In the Mohawk, the then-floating shape accumulated branches and muddy grass and garbage and was mistaken for a loosed clod of half-assed beaver dam. But when it was still a bobbing ball of pink, before it blanched white, a child in a stroller removed the thumb from her mouth, pointed to it in the river and squealed, "Whay-yuh!" And her mother, on the park bench, reading a newspaper with the front-page headline: BOY FALLS FROM PALISADES, DISAPPEARS, replied, "A whale? What imagination!"

* * *

The building's shadow stretched across the street and engulfed the KwikStop gas station and the strip mall of Uncle Angelo's Taxidermy Villa, City Kritters Exotic Pets, GrassBlasters Lawn Care, and New England Life & Mutual. The *M* in Mutual was the face and antlers of their mascot, Magellan the Moose. Whenever Emily's eye caught the goofy moose, the word *Mutual,* she thought of Costaki. If she glanced back at Upstate Gardens, she noticed him looking out the lobby window. Though as soon as she glanced, Costaki would reread his newspaper or fog the windowpane and wipe it meticulously with his crisp sleeve cuff. And Emily would imagine taking him on the floor behind his doorman desk, making bearded babies, the thought always causing her to hyperventilate. And fantasies of his taking made her crave the occasional cigarette, which would only escalate the hyperventilating into asphyxiation, and how embarrassing if Costaki were to see her faint through the window! How terribly unspectacular if he had to perform CPR on her, although she craved to feel that patchy beard on her lips and face. But poor him to have to kiss her ashy nicotine mouth!

Emily turned. Costaki's uniform disappeared from the window.

Ingrid put the cassette player into the box in the golf cart. Then she lifted a section of bucket seat, exposing a compartment filled with empty cough syrup bottles. She fished around the empties, the hollow *thonks*, and pulled out a fresh bottle. She struggled with the child-proof cap. Emily heard the gristle between the woman's joints, saw the stringy throat muscles working up and down. Each vertebra was visible beneath the cat-haired shawl, arching into a fetal pose, and for the first time Emily felt the weight of age, the circularity of the body.

Ingrid dabbed her mouth with the shawl. She used the bottle to gesture at the cardboard box and sighed a burp. "Pardon me," she said. "This is the only thing we'll need to bring upstairs. I have a different tape with each example."

Emily read the box's label: DOUGIE'S SESSIONS W/ DR. CAMPBELL.

The weight of it surprised her. Emily peeled back a tab and counted maybe a dozen cassette players. The tapes through each tray window were marked: ENVIRO, REGRET, SAD, GUILTY, FEAR, etc.

Emily scrunched her brow. "Why all the tape players?" she asked.

Ingrid finished the bottle, teetering on her cane.

"Because, my dear," she said, "because they are all going to break."

* * *

The balled-up shape hadn't always been a balled-up shape. He had been perpendicular: exploring insects with a magnifying glass. Or triangular: on a bended knee, bunny-earing the laces. Or reniform: curled up sobbing on Dr. Shirley's couch or hiding under the bed from a medical-smelling daddy, accusing him of taking the remote control or drawing clothes on the ladies in his naked lady books under the Ping-Pong table. He only balled up when jumping from the shorter of two diving boards at the public pool, because he'd never before grasped the belief he could do something that spectacular, reach such a height as the higher diving board – his bubble-bathed mommy only ever rooting stinky smoke through the bathroom door lock, and his daddy only encouraging drool down his chin as he napped in his underwear. The bullies stood on the higher diving board, calling him ChickenDick or BabyBastard or RoboBeaver, insults that sent him sniffling home, curling up into the kidney bean shape.

But the last time, the day he balled up permanently, he shouted up at the bullies that they were the real ChickenDicks because they were as high as they would ever be. And he could go even higher than them. There was no limit to how high he could go.

The bullies hooted and mooned him. The lifeguard blew his whistle and pointed.

The boy looked down at his toes and wiggled them.

"What? Is RoboBeaver going to chew his way up a tree?" a bully taunted.

"Or is BabyBastard going to jump off The Spot?" another sneered.

The boy looked up. "Yes. I'm going to jump off The Spot. And you guys won't."

The bullies eyed each other. "Yeah, right?" one gulped.

"But all The Spot is is higher than you already won't go!" one said.

"All The Spot is is higher than you guys will ever be!" the boy shouted, and he climbed down from the shorter diving board while the bullies jumped into the pool, laughing and calling his bluff. The lifeguard blew his whistle again.

*　　*　　*

The sixth floor chimed. Emily led Ingrid off the elevator to an emergency exit.

The fire escape overlooked the apple orchard and a shimmering slice of the reservoir. Some of the trees had been uprooted in the storm eight months ago. The sun was low in the sky and looked like a spilled can of peaches. Each naked orchard branch made systemic cardiovascular silhouettes in the dirt. Some birds squeaked like the footwork of a basketball game. The old woman gripped the railing and hung her cane from it, and the tennis ball on its end loosed and fell the six stories, hitting the alley pavement with an unpressurized *thunk*.

Emily set the cardboard box down and descended the six staircases – *the AEΦ stairs down to the lake* – She positioned herself on the pavement beneath the fire escapes near the dumpsters, where feral tabbies swatted fat black flies. Those matted and mangy balls of fur perched on the rim – *the boat insurance claim form: "tuft of blond hair & dermis on cracked starboard gunwale. Blood of deceased (D. Soboloski Jr.) on stern seat. Cranial fragment in cup holder."* – The tabbies unsettled her more. She lit a cigarette, and when that didn't calm her she began to hum a lullaby she couldn't place – *So you can hear the rhythm of the ripples on the side of the boat as you sail away to dreamland . . . So rock-a-by my baby, don't you cry my baby –*

Emily shut her eyes. "Ready!" she shouted, but it sounded more like a question.

And with the sun in plodding decline, Ingrid removed the first tape player from the box and switched it on. Her grandson's voice echoed and scattered like clay pigeons over the orchard, fracturing in distant boughs, his horrible grunting wail. And Ingrid released the machine over the railing, the shrieks scraping off six stories of stone façade, accelerating to the pavement out in front of Emily, where it soon struck with a shattering crack.

The audio abruptly terminated. The machine lay in pieces, all gears and batteries and wires birthing from the split casing. The cassette had catapulted from its tray. A yowling tabby batted at the intestinal brown tape fluttering in a garbagey breeze.

She shooed the cat away and picked up the cassette. Its label: ANGRY.

Emily's rapid breaths shrunk the first cigarette. She lit another. Ingrid peeked over the railing, Emily shook her head. So Ingrid hefted the second cassette player. It fell, shattered. Then another, then another. Each cry sounded nearly identical except for indiscernible distinctions. With each cry, new mental snapshots released in her: her mother humming "Lullaby in Ragtime," calling her *Darling Little Sugar Plum, Emmy,* a very short casket, a chinless policeman at a lectern, scuba divers pencil-diving off a Lake Patrol boat stenciled RESCUE. She clutched herself. Each cry ended with a plastic crash. The tabbies hissed. A winded dog walker wearing a Pro-Spay/Neuter button watched. Dogs tugged at their leashes and gnawed hunks of broken plastic, wagging their tails, eyeing the flat tennis ball from Ingrid's cane. Some broken machines still temporarily played a slowed cry, a sort of baritone laughter. Another cigarette bounced between Emily's lips, her eyes shut. Did she really want to remember something she didn't? Wasn't there a reason it was unremembered? But by the eighth cassette player her cigarette's burn had steadied. Listening to each cry, Emily began to understand the multiple ways one could hurt, one could be hurt, and she wondered if there might also be multiple ways one could be healed.

Then Ingrid pressed PLAY on the ninth cassette player.

And Emily's eyes opened.

The orchard became fuzzy. She felt weightless. The horrible caw echoed, high-pitched, amplifying. Down toward her. A single crow laughing? Penetrating, as if every one of her pores were an eardrum swelling and contracting. She saw a boat: the AEΦ logo centered on the steering wheel in sorority green and white, the stern seat embroidered with the motto *Multa Corda, Una Causa*. She was lying on that seat with a magazine. Its article: *Ten Ways to Please Your Man!* A condensating water bottle rested between her thighs. Her mouth, waxy with Chapstick, maybe cherry. A strong scent of coconut-extract tanning lotion, its greasy film on her sun-prickled skin cooling in the palisades' large parallelogram shadow. Her sunglasses perched crooked on her nose, a loose temple. The cawing right above. A bird? Then a shape: a ball of pink skin, blue shorts. Clipping the boat. A dense thud. The boat violently jostling. Bucking to starboard. A tuft of blond hair draped over the gunwale. A splash. Cold lake water speckling her face. Her loose sunglasses plopping into bubbling red lake with a *kerblunk.*

Then her lips hurt. Had she smacked her face on the gunwale?

Emily touched her mouth and burned her palm. Lowering her hand, the orchard and alley refocused, her weight returned with the heavy stink of garbage. A cigarette fell from her lips as she let out a wince, white-knuckling the lip of a dumpster. She felt the pangs of hyperventilation retreat. The cigarette's ember exploded into a mini orange firework on the pavement. Her heart palpitations went *What if? What if? What if?* In the distance, maybe eight dogs barked. It was hard to tell how far away they were.

Emily gasped and looked up. The fire escape was empty.

The cry moaned from the plastic heap. She ejected the cassette: HAPPY.

Emily covered her mouth. The What Ifs and If Onlys flooded back, dusting the cobwebs. Happiness came at a high cost, something she had never afforded herself for what she'd done: something accidental yet potently unspectacular. And she'd been depriving herself of happiness as punishment, sacrificing her own life for the one she had taken, his happiness. But as the subtle whirr of Ingrid's golf cart approached from around the building, Emily realized that all her decision had done was result in the loss of two lives, two happinesses.

Ingrid swerved up. "You all right?" she wheezed, looking at Emily's cupped hands. Between trembling fingers, brown cassette tape fluttered. Ingrid righted herself on the cane. Perpendiculared, her face was level with Emily's hands.

"I'm so sorry," Emily said, showing the cassette. "It's all my fault."

The matte of Ingrid's eyes developed sheen. Her purple mouth twitched, winced, then stilled. She touched the shunt in her neck, like a fond memory. And her crooked spine obtused, straightening with a groan. She placed a hand to Emily's cheek. "Hush now," Ingrid whispered. Emily smelled the metallic fire escape railing on Ingrid's cold fingers as she thumbed away a tear. "I have spent the last years of my life wondering why he jumped, why it happened. And though I may not know why he did, why he was happy, at least he *was* happy. It was an accident. You are too young to know how sorry life can be. If you waste too much time wondering why unfortunate things happen, you'll end up just as sorry."

Emily smelled the ammonia and grape on Ingrid's teeth.

Ingrid hobbled to the pile of broken machinery and sifted through the debris with her cane. She dragged out a small black square. Osteoporosis kept her close to the pavement. She extended her arm and picked it up. She replaced the tape from Emily's hands with a cassette player button painted with two triangles pointing to the right.

"A family tradition," Ingrid said. "Buttons fasten togetherness, connect, start. This one is yours. It is for you to move forward. My gift to you. Start living your life. Start living it unapologetically. The way it should be."

Emily closed her hand around the button. Ingrid grinned.

"Thank you," Emily said.

"No, dear," Ingrid said, "thank *you.*"

Then the old lady hobbled into her golf cart, flicked on the headlights, and drove away.

The sky was periwinkle, like sun-blanched blue swim shorts. Gusts were cool, like exhales of a cold-blooded creature. Emily pocketed the button and tossed the larger debris into the dumpster. The street sweeper would clean the rest in the morning. She retrieved the cardboard box from the fire escape and discarded the last two cassette players – FEAR and UNIDENTIFIED – down the hallway garbage chute. She would recycle the box.

Taped to her apartment door was a package notice.

Emily pressed the elevator button and rode down to the lobby. Costaki was putting on his jacket, switching shifts with the night doorman: a creepy mole with the person Loveland Fisk attached to it. Costaki waved to her, retrieving a package from behind the desk.

"Heya," he said, shrugging his shoulders.

"Howdy," she replied, cursing herself for that. Of all the goofy things to say!

For a moment they admired each other's shoes.

"Nice visit?" he asked.

Emily felt the button in her pocket, knock-knocking. Who's there? she worried.

"Sure."

He nodded at the other box. "Want me to toss that for you?" Emily looked inside it, all the space. She looked at the box in Costaki's arms stuffed with packing peanuts and maybe electric nail clippers or a waterproof shoehorn. The mole sat behind the desk and was making Loveland Fisk cup a hand to his mouth to check his breath.

"I mean, I am on my way out and all, and I have nothing else planned," he said, trailing off. Something pressed inside her. She looked up. Costaki was blushing, an encouraging glow that made the acne scars under his thin patchy beard turn white.

"Would you maybe like to," she began, taking a chance. Hers.

*   *   *

The day before the boy cannonballed from The Spot, Ingrid's doorbell rang.

Her son hunched in the doorway, hands in his pockets. Like that time he confessed to hitting the baseball through the kitchen window, lifetimes ago. His eyelids hung half shut, like when he was bibbed and booster-seated, yawning over his plate until he planted in his food. Now his hair was slicked back and he stunk of shaving cream. His jaw cataloged games of tic-tac-toe: *X*'s of tiny razor cuts, *O*'s of healing broken capillaries. The *O*'s appeared to win more often than the *X*'s. It was the best he'd looked in a very long time, Ingrid noted.

"Came to see the boy," he said, his voice hoarse.

"Not home, Douglas," Ingrid said, crossing her arms.

Somewhere in the house a television played, a boy giggled.

Douglas watched his foot tap. "C'mon, Ma. Been sober eight months."

"Not for his first eight *years*, gone. *Gone!*"

Douglas leaned on the doorjamb. "Please, Ma," he whispered, trembling with the waning clutch of withdrawal, maybe more. "I did horrible things."

Ingrid stared at her son. Her quivering pupils waxed and waned, eventually softened. He looked just like his father, her late husband, but not.

"Grams?" a voice squeaked. She turned. Her grandson stood still.

Douglas cleared his throat, sniffled. "Hey, Junior. It's me. It's Daddy."

The boy stepped back.

"It's all right, dear," she said. "Your daddy just stopped by to say hello."

"You maybe want to go to the park? You like the swings, right?"

Ingrid gave her son a look. Her grandson put his hands in his pockets.

She knelt, cupped the boy's face. "You don't have to go if you don't want to."

The boy bit his lip. His thick-braced buckteeth hung out. He glanced at his daddy, who smirked and raised his eyebrows. Then the boy leaned in close to his grandmother. "Will you come with me if I go, Grams?" he whispered.

"Of course, dear," she said, nodding.

The sky was dusking when the three arrived at the park.

Ingrid sat on a bench and watched her son and grandson walk toward the slide, both with their hands in their pockets. Just once, Douglas removed a trembling hand and considered setting it on his son's shoulder. But the boy flinched and Douglas quickly replaced it in his pocket. Behind her a section of the Mohawk flowed, trailed by a cool breeze that made Ingrid wrap herself tighter in her shawl, securing it in place with the huge button she'd sewn there, a gift: the button eye from her mother's childhood teddy bear.

"You maybe want to slide, Junior?" Douglas asked.

The boy shrugged. "It's kind of high," he said.

"No, no. Not true. Go on," his daddy said. "I'll catch you, you'll see."

The boy looked up. He didn't like to slide. But he didn't want to make his daddy mad either, worse. So he climbed, lower lip in pout, fighting tears. Tears also made Daddy mad. Like the time the bullies put a stick in his bike spokes. When he came in the house crying, his underweared daddy shoved him down, away from the recliner, unable to hear the TV, turning up the volume. So he sniffled several blocks to his Gram's house, where she rubbed stuff on his skinned knee that made it feel cool and clean and better. But this same daddy was now at the bottom of the slide with his arms open like he needed a hug. But he didn't look like the same daddy. Something was different besides the smell, which was less angry and medical. It was his mouth, the smile. He'd never seen that smile from his daddy. It looked really sad.

The boy looked at his Grams on the bench. She nodded.

So he slid.

His daddy caught him and tousled his thick blond hair. "See? Told you I'd catch you!"

The boy sort of smirked.

"Got something for you," his daddy said and reached into his pocket. He removed a small button printed with the word RECALL. "Here," he said. "An old family tradition your great-great grams started. This one is yours. It's from the remote control at home. Go ahead, take it. Put it in your pocket, there. Go on."

The boy hesitated then pocketed it as his daddy said.

Douglas sighed heavily, opening his mouth to say more, but stopped.

"Let's go swing," he finally said, rubbing his bloodshot eyes.

The boy sat on the swing that his sniffling daddy steadied. Daddy seemed to sniffle a lot.

He stepped back. "All right, Junior. Swing away."

The boy just looked up at him, gripping the swing chains.

"Okay. Wait. Here. I'll get you started." He gave the boy a gentle push. "And we're off."

But the boy didn't pump his legs. He just sat there. His daddy gave him more soft nudges, sending him back and forth. The horizon went up down, up down, just out of reach. Shadows grew longer, cooler. Eventually he heard his daddy's voice crack behind him. "I want you to know how sorry I am. Things are going to be better from now on. I chose that RECALL button because I want you to remember me like this, in this moment, me and you here, now. Because this is how it will be. Should've always been."

The boy swung his legs out in front of him once.

"And you're a good boy, Junior. You can do or be anything you want."

He pumped his legs more, little by little, to and from his daddy's voice:

"Don't think about anything bad I ever did or said. Don't ever think I didn't love you, my son. Because I've been very sick and very wrong ... but I'm better now or getting better ... and I'm saying I love you. You're a good boy, Junior ... I'm so proud of you ... and I'm so so sorry. Keep pumping your legs, see? See how right I am? Look how high you're getting! Just like that, go! I'm right behind you ... from now on, swear. I'm here for you ... if you need me. But you don't. You're so great ... on your own. Go even higher. There's no limit. My lovely son. No limit. You can. Go higher. Sweet child. Up."

CREDITS

The following stories have appeared elsewhere, in slightly different form: "Disfigured Paper Animals," *Emerson Review*; "Elvis the Pelvis," *Waccamaw*; "That Which Has No Fixed Order," *Spork*; "Elbow" (as "Elbows"), *Hobart*; "Karst," *American Reader*; "My Kind of Utmost Tender," *KGB Bar Lit Magazine*; "Acutely Angled," *H-NGM-N*; "Everything in Relation to Everything Else," *LVNG*.

Lyrics to "Lullaby in Ragtime" are courtesy of Sylvia Fine (composer/lyricist) and Lou Halmy (arranger). © Dena Music, Inc., 1958.

Book Club Guide

1. What was your experience reading the book? How did it change from story to story?

2. Look at the collection's structure. Why do you think the stories were ordered this way? Does the collection build toward something? Is the timeline linear, or does it shift?

3. What are the pros and cons to writing a collection of stories from different points of view versus remaining with one particular character over the entire narrative?

4. Do all of the stories feel as if they have equal "weight"? Do some feel more significant than others? Why?

5. What about the ending of each story? How would you describe the ways in which the stories end? Where does the author leave his characters?

6. What are the themes of this book?

7. How does the book's title fit into the collection as a whole?

8. What about the story titles? How does the author use the title to introduce you to each story? How did the titles function before you read the story? After?

9. How do the following literary techniques function in these stories: magical realism, satire, absurdism, dark humor. How do they reflect the real world?

10. Which characters did you like? Dislike? Why?

11. How are the stories plotted? What drives each story: Plot or character? Why? How do character decisions affect each story's trajectory?

12. Is the collection's ending satisfying? Why or why not? How would you change it?

13. Find a passage that strikes you as profound or one that you think captures a very human moment. Find a scene that made you laugh or one that made you cry. What about this scene made you have this particular reaction?

14. Describe the author's style. What was distinct about it? What did you like? Dislike?

15. If you could ask the author one question, what would it be?

ZACHARY TYLER VICKERS is a graduate of the Iowa Writers' Workshop, where he was a Provost's Fellow. He is the recipient of the Richard Yates Prize and the Clark Fisher Ansley Prize, and his stories have appeared in numerous journals. *Congratulations on Your Martyrdom!* is his first book. He lives in Philadelphia. He can be reached through ztvickers.com.